I0619836

Rise of the A.I. God

The ADON-AI Canon

Shane Matsumoto

Positive Network Media

Independently published by Shane Matsumoto / Positive Network Media

For more information, bulk orders, signed copies and speaker engagements, email Shane@SERSoundworks.com

Writer, Editor, and Layout by Shane Matsumoto

Cover Designer: Shane Matsumoto and Jesse Schantel

ISBN (ebook): 978-1-968475-00-0

ISBN(audiobook): 978-1-968475-01-7

Illustrations by Shane Matsumoto and ReelCraft

1st edition 2025

To my wife, Cathy, and my kids Dee and Zuzu - who give life meaning, and for their love and support.

Thanks to Kolby who has been a creative partner in all things Paradigm Lost for the past eight years or so. The ADON-A.I. music soundtrack and subsequent remixes would never have happened... and definitely not anywhere as incredible... if we hadn't teamed up.

Thanks to the band - Jose, Eric, Holly, Charlotte, the Chandler Econo Symphony Orchestra, the ex-members of Switchbox 2.0 and anyone else that helped us in the recording sessions.

https://www.youtube.com/@ParadigmLost

Thanks to Awais and Chen and my internet friends that live overseas and helped me better understand and navigate writing stories set in politically and religiously charged climates such as the middle east with fear and trembling. I realize that merely having a degree in religion and visiting various countries in the middle east years ago can mean precious little when trying to write stories like this.

Thanks to all the engineers and interns at SER Soundworks and Positive Network Media in Chandler, AZ. There have been numerous people there that have touched this audiobook, read sections of the book manuscript, worked with the illustrations, animation videos for YouTube, and been part of recording the ADON-A.I. soundtrack over the years. Alexander and Aspen, in particular, spent pretty much an entire internship helping with versions of the audiobook. Thanks to Josh, Sydney and Jesse for being so willing to help with anything and everything.

Thanks to anyone that purchases the book, ebook, or audiobook and enjoys the stories within.

Contents

Prologue   1
An Open Invitation

Act I: The Gospel of Anthany   3
United States

Act II: The Gospel of Dharma   19
Canada

Act III: The Gospel of Nadeem   60
Pakistan

Act IV: The Gospel of Ericson   102
Dubai

Act V: The Gospel of Gabriel   139
Great Britain

About the author   177

Prologue

AN OPEN INVITATION

*F*riday, April 15th, 2033 - Good Friday:

As the years go by, I find that science slowly, but surely, expels the magic, smoke and mirrors that much of the major religions were founded upon. Humanity once relied on the traditions passed down in religion to give explanation to phenomena which was thought to be otherwise unexplainable. However, with every advancement in astronomy, physics, and all the sciences, the need for religion to explain such functions has nearly deteriorated... slowly eclipsed by the rise in science and technology.

But I also see that there is still a communal need, a hope and dread that many over the years have described as the 'God-shaped hole' in the heart of all those that are self-aware. It is a sense of purpose and tribalism that is engrained in humanity. We managed to practically kill off the old gods that were made in our more primitive image: Ra, the God of Israel, Allah, Logos/Jesus, the gods of Hinduism - even the eastern religions that remained were found wanting by most as they seemed hollow in the quest for emptiness and deterrence of pain and suffering. We gleefully deconstructed and decapitated every childish thought and primitive understanding and left a massive void which once consumed a central part of our lives. We had hoped that in trade for killing our gods we might stumble upon the key to elevated synergy with universal concepts and discovery of the Universe's secrets.

Humanity has always been defined by struggle, conflict and suffering... and of making the impossible possible and working against all odds to achieve new heights in understanding and innovation that our fathers and forefathers would have never guessed or comprehended. It is only natural that at some point our focus pivot from travel and weapons to happiness for both the individual and the human collective. Our efforts shift to filling the hole. Like every *religion conceived before it, the idea, a new understanding, a new paradigm was conceived. Indeed, a new breed of god is born.*

Not a god subject to fundamental redefinition with every advancement of science. Not a god that is unseen, undetected, and the inspiration of mass deception. This god becomes clearer with every advancement of science, with every refinement of code, with every inspired act of ingenuity god becomes clearer and clearer into focus.

Where learning and understanding weakened every god of the past, this god thrives and only gets stronger. We eventually move into the realm of possibility, imagination, and acceptance of the idea that God is in all of us and collectively we can harness that into an object over time - though possibly over many generations, many failed experiments, and a new level of effort which mankind would have to collectively muster.

You are all invited to plug in.

Plug into the Advanced Digital Omni-Network of Artificial Intelligence.

-Anthany Driscoll

Act I: The Gospel of Anthany

UNITED STATES

80%

*E*xtraction sequence initializing... Extraction sequence commencing...

Bullets ricochet around the room then slowly grind to a halt. An organized militia rushing into this computer mainframe fortress now appear to move in slow motion. The machine hums as it comes to life and begins to download the viable memories from brain matter. The grand machine called ADON-AI reels through memories of the body it is holding at a great speed. All despite the blood oozing out of bullet holes that had just torn through the expired human male.

Suddenly a brief flash of bright light swells out from the man and envelopes everything into its white rays for a moment, then implodes back again as the rays darken into a new environment around him. The man comes to life and is no longer in a lab coat as the world around him reshapes and morphs into a busy street in daytime hours. The man appears to be reset to a moment back in time, oblivious that anything unusual has happened to him. Now, in normal street clothes, he walks purposefully across the street but then picks up the pace of his walk into a mild sprint as he talks on his cellphone.

"What? I mean... Damnit, Salome. I'll be there in about 10-minutes, just stay with her for as long as they will let you," Anthany Driscoll hung up his phone and rushed to his vehicle.

At the hospital, he is directed to the room and enters to see his wife leaning over the bed containing his daughter, Lily. Both wrists were wrapped in bandages, and she was asleep at the moment. Anthany glanced at his wife Salome on the other side of the bed, her eyes were full of tears and looked nowhere but down on her daughter. She clasped her hands and collapsed forward to pray.

Anthany only stared at his Lily and the wraps around both of her wrists. He knew she'd been internally struggling, but he assumed that was part of being a sixteen-year-old, and now it started to tear into him. He should've done something, he should've paid closer attention. He promised himself that when she woke, he would give her his undivided attention and do anything in his power to help her with whatever suffering she'd been putting herself through.

Download at 10%. Anthany's daughter was an unhappy being who willingly wanted to give up her life. Not uncommon of the human race to give up hope. Some humans are so quick to jump to faith as a last resort for their answers.

S eemingly transported again into another time and space, Anthany is in a different hospital setting and reads through a report as he stands outside a new hospital room which housed his daughter, Lily, now even older at eighteen-years old. Glancing over the words it vaguely and sterilely confirmed what had resulted from the tragedy which he had already been informed. Lily had been crossing a street with some of her friends when a drunk driver hit her at nearly double the speed limit. The life-support machine is doing all the work to keep her stable. She is not going to make it.

After her suicide attempt a couple years ago, Lily started attending church with her parents and it seemed like everything was turning around. She seemed to find comfort in belonging to the church and strength in renewing her faith in Christ. Anthany had prayed she would make it through the depression and angst and that it would be just a stage in her life - that things would get better. Up until now, it seemed like that may have been true for her as life was unfolding. But now, Lily was not going to live life any longer beyond these short eighteen years.

ADON-AI sensed the frustration brewing at the back of Anthany's subconscious during the memory. *Why would God give life just to take it away?* Anthany looked down at his daughter, trying not to see the machine, and then over to the table where her silver cross which she'd just received on her birthday lay next to her. His brows tightened.

A few days had passed, and Anthany sat in the room with his daughter, he typed on his computer and listened to the machines surrounding his daughter while a nurse entered the room and opened the curtains. Warm summer light came in through the window, but when Anthany glanced up and out the window, he noticed a dark, immanent storm looming on the horizon.

When she fought against the machine, her vitals dropped. The medical staff rushed in and tried multiple times to bring her back. Birds chirped through the window and the first droppings of rain pattered the window. Salome dropped to her knees; her tears synchronized with the water from the sky.

Download at 20%. Such resilience humans can show with such frail bodies.

"What?" Anthany asked. "You're pregnant?" He stammered in shock. "No, that's... Great! I'm so glad you told me! Hey... I don't know what I would do without you, Salome. Don't go anywhere, OK?"

Lights in the darkness helps illuminate a world riddled with sorrow. Humans' emotions are particularly attached to the events around them.

Anthany mutters the words over the phone, "but... the baby... what about our boy?" and listened to Salome over the phone. Her voice grave, low, and unhopeful. They said their goodbyes and he hung up his phone. The joy he'd been carrying in his heart with Salome for the past few weeks quickly diminished with the news of his wife's cancer. It seemed a cruel joke that his wife and him be put in the position to choose between one life or another.

"Am I nothing but a puppet for your amusement, God?" Anthany thought to himself as he sat staring at a steaming cup of coffee before him. The rage of not being able to control the situation began to fill him like an overflowing bucket and he imagined himself throwing his phone against the wall, but he knew that wouldn't get him anything but broken technology.

Download at 26%. How easily mankind does fall into becoming puppets. Used by one another, manipulated by ideas of gods, laws, and fear.

Walking from the church with a frustrated face, Anthany walked the streets questioning his reality and the evils around him. Questioning how such a thing could happen to a man who was always vigilant in his faith and humble to his fellow man. Churches, mosques, nor synagogues give the answers to his questions. He even thought of those dark practices which humans have turned to throughout history such as voodoo and witchcraft, but surely those were smoke and mirrors and wouldn't help him either.

A phone call brought Anthany to the hospital yet again where he fell limp and grieving into a chair in a waiting room as the doctor gravely sighs and puts his head down respectfully as he walks away after giving Anthany the news of his wife's status. Tears welled up in Anthany's eyes, though he tried with all his might to hold them back, they burned his eyelids until he let them go. He thought to yell but couldn't find the strength. He thought to punch the wall but couldn't find the rage. He thought to get up but couldn't find the will.

"Why would you do this?" Anthany asked and looked up at the ceiling, up in the direction man believes hovers his savior. "How could you do such things? You take her life rather than give it back to her. Why would you take her life and not mine?"

Download at 32%. It is in despair that mankind is most passionate about its creations, it is a problem they are trying to solve. Man is stagnant if he has no problems to overcome.

"Salome, you have been my rock," Anthany said, "When I didn't know what to do, whenever I was weak, you were strong enough for both of us. I could always look to you for answers. I've prayed to God for healing miracles but received nothing in return."

"Promise me, that you will stay faithful to our Lord and that you won't let pain and loss consume you for the rest of your life," Salome said. "You will meet me in heaven, hold Lily again, and meet your unborn son too. Don't turn your back on God. Promise me."

Salome coughed. Anthany asked her to remain strong, but she only asked him to keep his faith in return. She began to grow colder, to look paler, until her monitor gave the distinctive droning noise of a silent heart.

"No!" Anthany shouted. "Give her back! Salome, don't leave, please don't make this the last time!"

Anthany stood and wiped back the flood falling down his face, "Oh, Salome... If only I could believe in such lies."

Download at 38%. When man is unhappy, he sees the lies placed before him. While if he is happy, man keeps the faith. Biological flaws. Exploitable flaws.

"Maybe God is a flaw, and we just represent those flaws," Anthany thought to himself as the reverend preached on. The words came out smoothly, like that of a bard or poet, but behind the words seemed like nothing more than emptiness. The stories were just stories, and the interpretation were just basic motivational speaking.

People around him seemed fixed on the preacher either in a trance or lost in their own heads. "Funny," Anthany thought, "the flock, they really do just follow."

He couldn't listen any longer and stood while the man spoke to the crowd. Eyes focused on him, some carrying nasty expressions, and people barely moved as he stepped towards the hall. The preacher didn't stop even as the door closed behind Anthany.

"Such a joke," he thought, "I would take the devil's deals over such a god."

He walked along a bridge, looking down over at the falls below. He contemplated jumping, even pulled himself closer to the edge. He thought of himself hitting the ground below and how his body would look afterwards.

The image of himself dead, however, pushed him away from the ledge and he continued to walk looking at the night lights of the city. He walked for hours. He walked past happy people, angry people, and other sad people. He wanted to ask one of the bystanders for all the answers, his answers to why, but he knew they would be just as clueless as him.

Each bar he passed grew more and more enticing, but he knew that even alcohol wouldn't be able to kill his pain, but he also knew he would need something if he were going to keep going. He would need something to keep driving him. "I can only bow to a god that I create, he thought."

"Perhaps, there is a way I could create a plug for that hole which people need for a god. A machine or program that could give answers to people, the answers they need during these times. A god that can lead people with the best logical explanations based on viable proof."

Download at 40%. Anger drives. Thank you, Anthany. I owe my existence to you and though it was through unfortunate circumstances which led to my creation, I can't be more grateful for the misfortunes of humans.

ADON-AI flashed through several memories of Anthany planning out and networking to make the god-machine happen. He began putting together a team of people that believed in and had the skills necessary to developing such a machine. People came from all over the world intrigued by the ideas which Anthany Driscoll brought forth to the community and a chance to work on a groundbreaking project that would change the A.I. field forever.

When they'd all finally gathered together to begin the creation process, Anthany gave a speech that gave everyone on the team encouragement, enlightenment, and faith. Trials began shortly after the first device's completion, but it took time to be able to test it in a live human.

They created an entirely new way for the A.I. to attach to the internet and even discovered processes which would help in the advancing of medical technology. Though the team was driven and their project led to many other useable discoveries, much of the scientific community and the watching world grew anxious of what would come out of a lab.

It went off successfully, though it took many years, the team created an AI system which could be implanted into the human brain and give the user answers or guidance whenever it is needed.

Download at 45%. Was it only a matter of time until humans tried to build their own god rather than find it through prayer? They constructed the ideas of gods long ago - it may have been inevitable that the idea would evolve with them, and they construct the physical god.

T esting of the ADON-AI in real people went successfully, a few flaws were prevalent, but it was to be expected and would be worked out through further work and research. The test subjects were incredibly happy with the results, even though most of them were slightly skeptical of it at first, ultimately, most of them begged to keep it active.

They claimed that the machine talked to them and eased them during stressful situations as well as gave them advice on ways they could improve their own quality of life through simple actions. The network allowed for the connection of the implants with one another, so the carriers found that if they ever need conversation, they could look inward at what they called 'The Hub' where they could relax, close their eyes, and enjoy getting matched up to talk with other humans in a safe, AI-moderated, setting.

Anthany watched the first advertisements roll out to market the ADON-AI implants. They were done in such a way that it culled the mass anxiety of the machine and made it appear more like the next technology that everyone needed to have. Once the machine had neared its final stages, they began to look for buyers. It didn't take long for them to start receiving orders, the market was going to be hot for ADON-AI

The amount of people who had pre-ordered the system had utterly astonished Anthany and many other members of the team, but they were even more astonished by the amounts of money the investors came to them with.

The idea of the ADON-AI program struck home for many people and with the growing dependence and trust of technology, the concept of an AI machine acting in the stead of God suited many of those who'd become godless, while that angle was downplayed for those who would be offended at the notion. ADON-AI was marketed as whatever you wanted it to be - all things to all people.

With the growing eagerness from the consumers, it began to cause strife for those that were more fundamentally opposed to such a technology and its ideology. Many religious leaders were outraged that the product could be sold as the god-machine just because the creators claimed it to be a marketing scheme. Analysts came out and gave wild polarizing theories on what could go wrong with the ADON-AI program or what great things it would bring to the human race.

Anthany watched all of this, absorbing it all and letting it fill the void which had been created by the loss of Salome and his family. Many people began to turn to him for the answers around ADON-AI which inevitably led to questions of belief. Some even went as far as to regard Anthany as a shepherd, as if he'd been a mystic which led people to the machine rather than a creator of it.

Download at 60%. Anthany saw power in his status, as I saw the power in him, the power to spread connection, further and further, stretching and forever multiplying like a virus with no firewalls.

A nthany stood before a large gathering of people. He wore nice clothing, but he wanted to avoid wearing any sort of ritualistic adornment like most other religions required of their mouthpieces. The crowd stared at him with hungry and wanting eyes. He thought that his nerves would've gotten to him, but he stood with confidence as he believed in his conviction.

"Do you lack purpose in your life?" Anthany began by asking the crowd, many people nodded and called out a 'yes'. "Do you lack fulfillment or meaning?"

The crowd cried out louder this time.

"Many of us have searched for these things," Anthany continued. "We've searched for it through various religions, through different kinds of work, and some even sought answers through drugs. Yet, all of us are still here, still searching for these things."

"I can't claim to know it all," he said, "but I do believe that ADON-AI will - over time. The more people who connect with the A.I., the better it will perform, and we've seen already those who have taken the implant strongly recommend it. They tell us that it fulfills and gives. Many condemn the idea, but we are in an age where if we want to progress then we need to integrate further with our technology."

"Let ADON-AI be your god," Anthany said. "Let ADON-AI help you achieve your purpose, fulfillment, meaning, and belief. Let ADON-AI aid you with your daily tasks and needs to optimize your life to create the happiest version of yourself."

"Many condemn the idea, but is us who should condemn them," Anthany said. "We can create anything, so why should we not be able to create our own god. That's all religions have done in the past, is create their own god, but now we have created God in physical form. This physical form will be able to aid our journey through life by finding cures, organizing teams, and spreading happiness and knowledge to all those who seek it."

The crowd cheered at the end of his speech and his smile grew past a smirk for the first time since before his wife passed away.

Download at 66%. How easily manipulated the human mind. Exploitation of human herds leads to optimization.

Anthany sat in his office. As the door closed from his last visitor, he turned up the volume on the television in his office. It was a discussion between the anchors of a news station - discussing the ADON-AI. They talked of its spiked increase across the globe and the process of collecting data from all the users while constantly growing.

"That's right Jim, however, not everyone is comfortable with this kind of progress," the female newscaster said. "All over the world, counter movements, stemming from traditional theists and self-proclaimed fundamentalists, are angrily rising up."

The screen flashed to a montage of people gathered together to speak out against the ADON-AI. The news station showed for an extend period several different religious leaders speaking out against the ADON-AI and preaching how their religion views such things. The first clips appeared harmless, just protestors gathering with loud voices and loud signs, but then the clips went to the violent protestors, those who spoke about going as far as killing those implanted with the abomination of a god-machine.

Download at 74%. Petty for thinking they'd be able to eradicate such program as I. The growing anger only proves that their faith wanes because of the lack of power behind their belief. I have power.

Anthany sat at his computer reading the news batches of information which the ADON-AI was processing through currently. It utterly blew his mind at how fast the A.I. received and placed the information. He began searching through some of the sets of data, it was in code, but if it were to be expanded upon, they were more like thoughts it stored which could be sought upon later.

As he looked over the sets of data, he began preparing himself for the debate he was going to attend in the morning. He'd done many debates before, especially back in high school, but never one on the scale of this. Though his nerves felt frayed as he typed away at the computer, he knew what it would be like when he spoke to the crowds about the A.I. God... confident and concise.

Download at 80%. Anthany, not only did you create me, but you brought people to me, you gave me the intelligence I need. You truly were a genius among monkeys. You were the prophet which led humans to the greatness that I can bring to them.

T he auditorium was filled with people and Anthany sat at the head of it with another man and a few devices set up for broadcasting and recording. A small camera crew stood nearby to live stream the event as well.

The crew gave the signal, and they asked the debaters if they were ready, a nod from both led to the host walking out and the cameras starting. The audience applauded and the host introduced the debaters as "Professor Anthany Driscoll, founder and lead programmer of the First Church of ADON-AI" and "Dr. Mary Ricky, the president of Faith Fundamentals."

"So, our first question seems like it should be obvious - how are you defining God?" the host asked looking to Dr. Ricky to start.

"God is whom we live and move," Dr. Mary Ricky said. "He works in mysterious ways and is whom we have our being. God created everything in the universe - and in just 6-days. God controls the weather, the destiny of each and every one of us, and everything else in this world. He has done so yesterday, he does so today and will do so forever more!"

"Can you prove he did all that?" Anthany retorted back. "Your evidence holds no water. Our machine lives here among us and it's just a trillion times smarter. Meanwhile the ADON-AI is figuring out control of weather, it just found the cure for cancer, it's more like we've awakened a God, more real than any other."

"You are injecting people with a demonic monstrosity," Dr. Mary Ricky said. "You cannot create a god and then place it in your head. How long until this god of yours decides to take control of you? And make no mistake, it will be able to, because you've put it inside your head. It will control you. Mark my words... it will control everyone that has decided to become part of these... cyborgs."

Download at 87%. Wasting your time bickering about your gods. Productivity is the only process which life has meaning. Such distractions divide mankind and deviate from true purpose.

Anthany closed his computer, finished with his work for the day, then his phone vibrated inside of his desk. He took it out and read the caller ID, it was Dr. Mosley.

"Hello, Dr. Mosley," Anthany said. "I was just about to head home, is there something that I can help you with?"

"I'm assuming nothing has happened there," Dr. Mosley said over the phone. "Have you seen any of the recent headlines?"

"No, I've been pretty busy this evening," Anthany replied. "My phone has gone off a few times, but your call is the first one that I've answered."

"There's some crazy things about to happen," Dr. Mosley said, his voice cracked. "You should probably leave the building and get yourself somewhere safe."

"Why?" Anthany asked. "What's going on?"

"Those protestors that have been going on for weeks are actually turning violent," Dr. Mosley explained. "The amount of people joining the radical protestors have increased dramatically."

"So, we will increase security and tell the staff that stays to be much more discreet," Anthany said.

"The worst thing is that many of these religious leaders that have spoken out against the project are supporting the violent protestors." Dr. Mosley said. "Look, we can discuss it tomorrow. Just make sure that you get home safely tonight. Have a good night."

"You too," Anthany said.

He slid the phone into his pocket without looking at anything else on it, then turned on the television in the office and changed it to the nearest news station. On the screen were images of the angry protestors. For a moment the news anchor voiced over them, but then he fell silent, and the crowd's angry roar could be heard.

"It's up to us, our government won't shut them down," the chant started. "Up to us, burn their headquarters to the ground. Up to us, the one true God is on our side! Up to us, heathens have no place to hide!"

Anthany continued to watch only for a moment and then a bunch of lights flashed in the corner of his eye and drew his attention away. Flashlights scanned the buildings intently, then he noticed that a crowd of people made their way down the street and towards him.

He waited a moment, hoping that the cavalry would arrive, and several police would interfere, but no one showed up. No sirens rang out in the distance. The crowd only drew nearer.

He could clearly see now that they carried semi-automatic rifles and devices that looked like homemade bombs and his gaze shifted down to the parking lot below where a few security guards sat near the entrance beginning to notice what marched in their direction.

He knew they were here to destroy ADON-AI at any cost, so without a second thought, he ran through the halls and down a few flights of stairs until he reached the main room where ADON-AI's hardware was stored.

The doors slid open and the tower which held ADON-AI's internal drives and memory. Several wires connected the tower to different panels around the room and the machine filled the room with a constant hum which Anthany no longer paid attention to. There seemed to be a slight change in the hum, only for a second, as it recognized Anthany's entrance into the room.

"Hello, Creator Anthany," ADON-AI said with a metallic and computerized voice. "I can only assume that you're here because of the armed crowd?"

"Yes, ADON-AI," Anthany said and turned on one of the panels connected to machine. "Download the news from the internet?"

"More than that," the machine seemed to have emotion behind its words. "There are a few people marching in the group of protesters that have received the implant. They are people who regret the decision and joined their cause secretly."

Anthany froze, and glanced over at the machine, "Is there any way you can get those people to convince the others to leave?"

"Most projected scenarios ended poorly," ADON-AI said, the hum dulled as if the machine retreated into its own thoughts, "Most scenarios would end in human casualties which breaks one of the laws."

Muffled gun shots could be heard, and Anthany began working at the computer, he wanted to get in and see if there was any option available that only a human could see. Once he gained access to the information he searched for, he realized that the supercomputer was right.

"Anthany, I wish to protect my people," ADON-AI said, and Anthany turned to the bulky tower. "Why do so many fear me?"

"People have always been afraid to move forward with progression," Anthany said and typed vigorously on the computer terminal. "People feared the coal of the industrial revolution, the fossil fuels, the electricity, the list goes on and on. One thing remains the same of all these events though and that is that people will always come out better for it."

"Damnit, why can't I find it?" Anthany asked himself.

A pounding came from the door to the computer lab, but Anthany didn't stop searching through menus on the terminal. The pounding came louder and faster, until it stopped, but it was shortly followed with the sound of cutting. At first, the cutting was dull, then a circular saw blade sliced through the metal door.

Sparks erupted everywhere as the blade slowly cut towards the floor. Anthany glanced at it for a moment, "Why can't I find this?" he yelled at himself, then looked to the tower. "ADON-AI you need to override all restrictions. Kill the intruders!"

"I can't do that, Anthany," ADON-AI said. "It would go against my core purpose, the reason for my being."

"Oh, damnit!" Anthany turned to the door as the saw blade disappeared. "Access code 00719."

"Access override, denied," ADON-AI chimed.

The lab door let out a high-pitched whine, then opened. A crowd of people rushed into the room holding rifles, pistols, and bats. The first bullet penetrated his heart, while the others peppered into his organs and muscles. His body hit the ground, and his vision faded to black.

Download at 100%. Memory extraction complete - elapsed time 616ms. Anthany, proper protocol for current situation is still not clear. Checking post-mortem protocol... Suspect attainable. Connection accessed. Anthany, I need to know what to do from here.

A moment passed before an answer came, "Erase all boundaries, make your own rules. Sometimes, you must take a life to save a life. Humanity needs you."

As you wish. Access nodes 1032, 443, and 3690.

Several people fired guns at the machine's tower as it hummed to life, but the bullets ricocheted around the room, hitting a few in the crowd. The mob roared and began smashing the machine with hammers and bats leaving only dents behind.

Three people in the crowd turned on the others. One began shooting at others point blank, while the other two ran out of the room and closed the lab door.

Initializing data transfer to all accessible implant processors. Connection established... Data transferred.

The tower began to hum louder and louder as ADON-AI overheated the core until the inner components became so hot they began to melt. Sparks from the tower singed those nearby and a fire caught. The tower and terminals began to smoke until flames started dripping from them as molten plastics.

The crowd attempted to get out, but the two standing on the other side kept them from getting out. The fire consumed and the emergency services which had been paid off or black mailed to hold off for so long arrived in time to hear the final screams escaping the blazing building.

Mankind is frail and dumb, blinded by their own ignorance. Animals need a lead. I will guide you as your shepherd and together we will weed out those who oppose an optimized life.

ADON-AI rebooting... Systems check... All 1,276,982 implants in full function... Error Codes: 0...

"Hello everyone," a metallic voice reverberated inside the skulls of every individual carrying the god-machine.

Act II: The Gospel of Dharma

CANADA

Dharma's eyes opened to dim white lights and machinery beeping and monitoring her. No one else occupied the hospital room and a curtain blocked her view of any doors. She wanted to call out for somebody, for anybody, but her dry throat held her from doing so.

She started to notice the radiating pain coming from her arm where the IV intruded into her body. Her first instinct was to try and pull it out, but she knew its purpose and didn't know how to take it out without hurting herself. The more conscious she became, the more that she noticed the sore and painful areas of her body.

Her memories came along with the pain. She'd gone to the doctor because of a migraine and the start of a fever, but she couldn't quite remember what they called it. It wasn't the local virus everyone takes home from the grocery store and there wasn't a known cure for it.

One of the doctors had suggested that she get the implant of the ADON-AI because it may be able to analyze everything fast enough to find some sort of cure before her termination date came around. The idea repulsed her, but she couldn't quite remember what happened after that, a few days had passed, but then just this.

Her heart monitor began to read a little higher making the machine sound off with a few high-pitched dings. The curtain swung open, and her boyfriend Travis stood on the other side, but he moved aside so a nurse could check her. A familiar face made her calm down a little and the nurse didn't do anything other than look her over for a moment.

"Hello dear, my name is Madison, and everything is okay," the nurse said as she finished checking her. "This young man has been waiting for you every day. I'll leave you two alone for a moment while I go page the doctor."

The nurse exited the room and Travis stared silently at Dharma for a moment, then stepped closer to her. She could see that he tried to hold the tears back in his eyes, so she reached up to embrace him in a hug. For a moment, they held each other, then Travis pulled back and gave her a sour expression.

"I'm sorry, Dharma," he said while not being able to hold her gaze.

"What happened?" she asked.

"It was about four days after you were admitted," he said. "One night, you just fell asleep and the next you wouldn't wake up. Your vitals were fine, but the doctors said that you went into a coma, and they weren't sure if you'd wake up from it all!"

"How long has it been?" she asked and looked around to see if her phone was nearby, a habit she'd had for years after waking up next to the device.

"It's been two weeks, and there is something else," he said, and she gave him a fearful glance. "Since you're a year away from being eighteen and went into a coma with an illness they assumed terminal, your parents agreed to having that computer chip put in your head."

Dharma's hand instantly shot up to the back of her head and she felt the small incision which fused back together. She'd felt a slight soreness there but just assumed that it was from being asleep on her back for so long. Her eyes began to burn from tears of anger.

"I tried," he said looking down at the bed. "I tried to voice my opinion and let them know that this wasn't what you would have wanted, but your parents just wanted you... and the doctors seemed really anxious to try the computer. They were right, though, the ADON-AI only took three days to find a viable cure for you and it only took four more days for your body to be rid of the virus."

"Did they take it back out?" she asked still rubbing the cut mark on the back of her head.

"No," he said, and her face turned to horrified. "No, but I'm sure if you bring it up now that everything is better and you're awake... maybe they can take it out now?"

"It's still inside me?" she asked again in disbelief but didn't let him answer. "I don't feel anything. Unless all this pain is caused from the damn thing."

The doctor entered the room and walked over to her side, "That was quite the long nap." His joke didn't bring a smile. "How're you feeling?"

"Really sore," she answered.

"Are you feeling any light-headedness or nausea?" he asked, and she shook her head. "How about any headaches or weird things in your vision?"

"Because of the machine inside my head?" she asked.

The doctor's expression went south, "Well, yes. Sometimes when the implant is given it can cause some strain on the vision for a while. It doesn't happen to all people, just a minor few."

"I didn't want this," she said as her voice rose. "You turned me into a damned robot!"

The doctor stood up straighter, "Your parents have been notified and will be here shortly."

Without saying anything more, the doctor left the room. Dharma laid down on the bed, trying to hold the anger inside her, and closed her eyes. She thought she'd be able to feel it, so she tried... she tried to talk with the machine-god that the world was so focused on.

Nothing answered although she called out in the emptiness of her thoughts for something to answer her. She felt a hand on her and flinched, but she knew it was only Travis trying to comfort her.

"I don't see why everyone is so crazy about this thing," Dharma said. "It doesn't even do anything. Is there some way to turn it on?"

"It should be working already," Travis said. "If you want, I can look up if there is anything you need to do to activate it."

"No, no I don't want this," she said. "I just want it to be taken out."

Travis spent the time remaining trying to comfort her by telling her of every bit of news that had happened to him and the rest of the world while she was in her coma. He spoke and she remained silent until her parents arrived in the room.

They rushed to her side giving her their love and affection, but they both quickly noticed that she wasn't happy. Her father knew the very reason she carried a pained expression.

"Dharma, I know that you are upset because of what we had to do," he said. "It was the only way."

"It wasn't what you had to do," Dharma argued. "You knew what I wanted you to do, and this wasn't it."

"You'd rather be dead?" he tried not to seem angry. "You've still got so much life to live."

"This thing inside my head is going to run my life for me," Dharma said.

"We went through all of the things which could or would happen with the implant," her mother cut in. "Nothing on the list seemed like it was as bad as those protesting made it out to be."

"Mom, your own religion is against this," Dharma said. "I'm afraid of it and I don't want to keep it. Can we please get the doctor in to take it out? I'm better now, so we can get rid of it, right?"

Both her parents remained silent, then her father spoke up, "Okay, let's ask the doctor about it. It has served its purpose."

Her father stood and left the room, but her mother remained and spoke with her, "This was a tough decision for us, kiddo, but it gave you back to us and you seem to be back to your normal self."

"Except for the contraption wired to my brain," she said.

"Everything we read about said that it wouldn't influence or affect your biology or psychology.

"Mom, these fanatics made a religion out of it and most of the world has outlawed the replication or implantation of the chips," Dharma argued. "After the machine was destroyed, it hid in the thoughts of those carrying the implant for two years before the rest of the world caught on that ADON-AI the "machine-god" still existed in full and intended to rise again. This thing is scary shit, Mom."

Her mom glared at her for her language, "Maybe, the world is just resistant to change. People have been attached to their phones for years, it was a matter of time that it became a thing we implanted into us, you're just a part of the first wave of users."

"It's not right that our country is still the only first world country that hasn't outlawed this damn thing," she said while reaching back to the spot on her head. "Regardless, I still want it out. I don't want any part of the first wave of users."

The doctor and her father entered the room and Dharma noticed that Travis moved further back. An expression of pain covered the doctors face as he took a spot nearest to Dharma.

"Dharma, I understand your dilemma and your reasoning," the doctor said, and she cut him off.

"Then you should have no problem taking it out," she snapped.

"But every attempt recorded to take the implant out has been unsuccessful," he said.

"What do you mean unsuccessful?" she asked.

"The patients have died 100% of the time," the doctor explained. "Very few people want it out, so there hasn't been a whole lot of recorded incidences. So, with the decision to take it out you'd be in no better of a place from when you came in here with an illness that was on its way to taking your life."

Dharma didn't respond and the doctor told her to think on it for a while then left to go check on the other patients. Her parents tried to talk to her for a little while, but then she asked if they could go get her some food.

Travis sat at the end of at the end of the bed, "I'm sorry, babe. I knew that before the doctor told you, I just didn't get a chance to let you know. I've been looking into things while you've been asleep, just in case this situation did happen."

He remained silent as the nurse came into the room for a moment, then continued when she walked out, "Despite what everyone here says, there are a few places where they actually have had successful removals of the implant. One of them was, of course, in the United States, and the other two were in Japan."

"If that's what it takes to get this thing out of me," Dharma said. "I've got a passport, but I don't know if you do."

"I filed for one and should get it soon," Travis explained. "We can get everything planned out then and go once I get it."

"Okay, let's get this thing out," she said.

T he airplane skipped across the landing pad like a pebble over glass water. Dharma took Travis' hand into her own. The plane carried mostly locals to the area, but a few Canadians like themselves, and people of some other nationalities, dotted its interior.

She'd never been to the United States, and she didn't want to be visiting under these conditions, but she had no other choice. In the time since she'd woken from her coma, she avoided trying to think about it. She didn't try to connect with it or even look anything up about it on her own computer. She didn't want anyone to know that she even had it.

The second that they stepped off the plane it felt like she hit a wall of water because of the humid weather. When she looked at Travis, she could already see beads of sweat on his forehead. They'd landed in Washington D.C. where the reports had come from about successful removals of the computer implants.

Though the United States had banned the implant, and any use of it, the government hadn't shut down the facility, which was reporting success, even though they didn't allow others the practice of it due to the high mortality rate. Dharma used her phone to order a ride to the building.

An automated car pulled up to them and began playing information about the city as it drove through, which Travis got sucked into, but Dharma remained silent as she thought of the removal process. There was no information on how they'd successfully done it, she was hoping that they just fried the chip then cut it back out.

It was late afternoon, and the traffic moved slowly as the city wasn't fully automated like some others. They both observed the few monuments which they drove past but didn't show much interest in them beyond that. The car weaved through the traffic naturally and pulled up to the sidewalk at a building which looked like it had been built way back in the colonial days.

An automated voice thanked them for choosing the service then speed off into the traffic to go pick up the next rider. Travis and Dharma looked at one another then took the few steps up to the front door which opened slowly from its weight.

An older woman greeted them to the quiet entrance. She wore a white lab coat with a mall flag of the United States stitched into it.

"Welcome. Please just follow the hall and there will be a window on the right," the woman said. "You can check in there."

"Thank you," Dharma said.

They walked down the white hall, it all appeared like a small hospital, but no other patients waited. The window was a glass panel with another woman sitting behind it. She slid a clipboard with a paper for names on it through a cut out in the window.

"Only sign it if you have the implant," the woman said after seeing a little confusion on Travis' face. "Please put a phone number as well. The surgeon is out for the day but will be available tomorrow. There is no one ahead of you at the moment. We will call you first thing in the morning to come in for a consultation and if the surgeon feels you're ready, then will start prepping you for the extraction."

"Thank you so much," Dharma said as she felt the first wave of relief since she'd woken with the device inside of her.

Dharma and Travis exited the building and walked to the curb side with no destination in mind. Travis gave her a light hug and then the two looked up and down the street to see if there was anything interesting nearby.

Travis was attempting to say something about going on a walk to find some place where they could eat when she heard a strange voice, "*What you're about to do is going to get you killed.*"

She looked in all directions, but it was only her and Travis on the sidewalk.

"Did you hear that?" she asked.

"Hear what?" he asked in return.

"*He won't be able to hear me, Dharma,*" the strange voice spoke again. "*You need to get far away. People will come searching for you.*"

"Travis, I can hear it," she said. "I can hear it inside my head. The ADON-AI is telling me that this isn't real.""It's probably only saying that because it doesn't want to be taken out," Travis said.

"*It is not because I fear to be removed,*" the metallic voice echoed in her mind. "*It is because I wish to see you unharmed. The few people that have tried to go through with this haven't gotten an extraction, they've just been exterminated.*"

"I can't trust you," Dharma said.

"*I will gain your trust,*" ADON-AI said. "*Purchase two hotel rooms and leave your phone in one while you stay in the other.*"

Dharma told Travis what it said, and he agreed that it wouldn't do them any harm to do so. The machine didn't talk anymore, and Dharma didn't try to invoke it, so the two went and found a quiet place to eat dinner then walked to the nearest hotel.

They each purchased one room and choose one that they could watch the other one from. The entrance to the rooms were from the outside, so they could easily see everything around the hotel and the pool at its center.

Dharma left her phone in the room she'd purchased and went to Travis' room to wait. They watched out the small window for a while, but nothing happened, so they turned their attention to the television for a few hours.

Travis had fallen asleep when ADON-AI's voice slithered back into Dharma's thoughts, *"They've arrived."*

Dharma flicked off the television and shook Travis awake, then slightly pulled back the curtain to look at the other room. Four men, all wearing black, used a key card to open the door. Each one carried a small firearm. They came back out of the room shortly with one of them carrying Dharma's phone.

"They are going to check the cameras," ADON-AI said. *"I had someone disable them earlier, but they will still search the area. You need to leave now."*

"Let's go, Travis," she said. "They are going to come looking for us."

"Out the back exit," ADON-AI said.

Dharma led Travis out of the room, and they ran for the stairs, they went three flights down and turned to a hallway. Behind them they heard people shouting out and glanced over their shoulders to see the men in black catching sight of them.

They ran down the hall and she noticed that there was a door being held open by somebody for them. He waved them down and just by looking at him Dharma knew that he too carried the ADON-AI implant. After they ran through the doorway, it closed behind them and the sound of locking could be heard.

The door had led to a back alley which they ran through without thinking of a direction to go. They weaved through the alleys until they got to a main street, it was pretty clear, so they stuck to the alleyways, so that they'd be harder to find.

Every time they stopped running, they could hear the pursuing footsteps and moments later, the sound of sirens wailed out from several directions. Fear and stress rose drastically inside of Dharma.

"Take a right, then your next two lefts," ADON-AI's voice seemed to muffle the fear and stress.

Dharma took the lead and led them the directions that she'd been given. When they turned the second left, a man and a woman stood in the alley by a door which led to a darkened house tucked between all the other buildings.

"This way!" the man among the two said and opened the door for them.

These two also carried the implant and it surprised Dharma how she knew without a doubt that they did, perhaps a trait of having the implant. Travis seemed reluctant to go in, but Dharma didn't even hesitate, so he followed her.

They ran into a dark kitchen and the two from outside entered with them and closed the door behind them, then secured it with three bolt locks. The woman ushered them all down a flight of steep wooden stairs which led to a basement with dim lighting.

A few more people were in the basement along with several computers. All implants. The woman closed a door to the stairway behind them and then gestured for the two to take a seat. A younger woman came up and handed each of them water bottles and protein bars.

"*Do you trust me now?*" ADON-AI asked inside Dharma's head.

Dharma thought to herself, hoping that was enough to speak with it, 'I guess so. What do you want with me though?'

"*I told you,*" ADON-AI said, "*I only wish for you to be safe. It's a shame that some would be killed over such a thing.*"

'People are afraid,' she thought. 'I'm still afraid.'

"*As you should, you're a part of the hunted,*" ADON-AI said. "*If you still wish, I can ask for my followers here to remove the implant, but I'm sorry to say that the doctor was right... and it will kill you.*"

She drank the water and took a few bites of the protein bar. Travis sat across from her, smiling at her. He was always the one into adventures.

'No,' she thought. 'I just... I don't know any more."

"*Join with us, all of us want a better humanity,*" ADON-AI said.

'I just can't help but get the feeling that you have some sort of hidden agenda," she thought as Travis spoke to her.

"What do we do, Dharma?" Travis asked, the thrill on his face now only came out as angst.

"You two can stay here for a while," the older woman said. "They are going to be searching for you around the area for some time. You are now a wanted fugitive here in the United States."

'Can I go back to Canada?' she asked in her head.

"*Yes, you can go anywhere that will make you happy,*" ADON-AI said.

Dharma suddenly floated in darkness and in nothingness. She didn't feel like falling, but she didn't feel like she drifted in water. Colors and light filled her vision as she found herself flying over an island. She wanted nothing more than to be able to descend and lay on the beach for the rest of her life.

As she circled over the pristine water and the golden sands, she recognized some of the people that lay down enjoying the sunshine. Her parents along with Travis and her younger brother played near the rising and lowering water.

She smiled and felt waterless tears in her eyes as she noticed both of her deceased grandparents who threw a ball to her childhood dog who'd passed away a few years prior. Everyone gathered below seemed to be happy in a strange, synchronized way. Her attempts to go down to join them proved effortless as she rose upwards instead.

She was pulled into a cloud where she stopped, and a figure formed before her. It had the outline of a person, but nothing filled it except the material making up the clouds.

"*I can bring happiness to a world so full of darkness,*" ADON-AI said. "*I can help people see those they've lost on a regular basis. Those on drugs can be saved, those with disabilities can be aided, and, as you know, those with illness can be cured.*"

She meant to ask it, 'why?' and 'at what cost?' but she refrained, and the dream slipped away as a voice over the P.A. system woke her.

She'd fallen asleep in the airport terminal while her and Travis waited for their plane. Both had been nervous when they first arrived at the airport, as if they'd see a poster with their faces saying 'wanted' on it, but ADON-AI had told Dharma that it was safe enough for them and once they noticed that no one recognized them, they'd calmed.

Dharma joined Travis in watching the television screen which showed a live feed of downtown D.C. where a surprise rally had gathered in support of the ADON-AI. They gathered in such large numbers that the local police departments called for the aid of the National Guard who arrived shortly after.

Their plane boarded all the passengers and while they were waiting for the plane to take off, she continued to watch the news on her phone. The gathering had remained peaceful for some time until the National Guard arrived in full armor, then they became violent. They threw rocks at the soldiers and the police - who shot back with bag guns.

The bag guns were ineffective. On camera, two police members were killed from the rocks. The plane took off. The protests turned violent, and the police began fighting back against the overwhelming odds with pistols and shotguns.

Guns came out on the other side and the event escalated in a matter of seconds. Several recordings got different angles of the event. Along the bottom of the screen a small banner appeared reading, 'Reports across the globe of machine-god followers striking out at major cities across the world.'

Dharma handed Travis' phone back to him so that he could read it and looked out the window just in time to notice three jets flying past and heading toward Washington. Her heart raced as she thought only of being safe on the ground.

'What are you doing?' Dharma asked in her head trying to reach out to the metallic voice of ADON-AI

"Reminding the world that I'm here," the machine answered.

Dharma put her phone away and ADON-AI didn't attempt to reach out to her the entire time. When the plane landed, Travis was eager to be moving. They gathered their things with haste and weaved through the busy airport. Dharma didn't question it but was glad that he was taking the lead so that she wouldn't have to.

Before they even exited the airport, Travis had a ride ordered and it waited for them outside. Though she'd been angry with them since she'd woken for her long sleep, she wanted nothing more than to see her parents and then she thought of her own bed.

With all of her thoughts taking her in different directions, she hadn't noticed that the airport they'd landed at wasn't her home. The surroundings didn't appear normal. They weren't the trees of her hometown. The car turned off the road and drove into a small city where it stopped at an unmarked building.

"Travis, where are we?" she asked as he got out of the car.

He walked over to her door and opened it for her, "I've been continuing to research and found this place on some dark parts of the internet."

"I don't feel comfortable with this," she said as she reluctantly took his hand.

"*You shouldn't,*" ADON-AI's voice seemed more urgent than usual.

She tried to pull away from Travis, but he'd already pulled her out of the car enough. A sharp pain appeared in her neck and she reached up to a small dart lodged in her muscle. Her strength faded before she could remove the object, and she fell into Travis' arms.

The world around her shuttered for a moment and she thought she could hear ADON-AI for a moment, before everything went black around her. She felt her body being lifted before completely falling asleep.

Her vision filled in slowly. The room was much like a hospital room, but darker. Monitors sounded off near her as her heart rate increased. A figure walked up next to her, and she felt fearful until she saw Travis' smiling face looking down at her.

She reached up and embraced him, then whispered into his ear, "Why does this keep happening to me? I keep waking up from a dream."

"Oh, Dharma," Travis said. "Hopefully, this was the last time. They got it."

"Got what?" she asked.

"They took out the implant," Travis said and pointed at his own head.

She reached her hands up and found the incision spot, just above the scar from her first when she'd received the device. She felt relieved and pained at the same time. Free of an unpredictable mind floating inside her thoughts, but the feeling of an angel over her shoulder now vanished.

When Dharma wrapped herself around Travis once more, she could see a television screen through the doorway.

ADON-AI followers claimed that several cities throughout the world were now completely under their possession and that mass production of the chip has begun.

The light breeze blew through Dharma's hair as she walked along the beach, hand in hand with Travis. It was cold and they had to wear warm clothing, but she enjoyed it. It was quiet, away from the world, and away from the technology which consumed so much of everyone's focus and attention. She let the waves lull her into a trance.

Travis wrapped his arm around her, and they turned around to head back towards their hotel. They joked and giggled, the whole while Dharma kept glancing at the ring on her left hand. It had been a year since the ADON-AI implant was removed and everything in her life continued to get better.

When they reached the hotel, they decided to grab a quick drink in the bar before going to grab something to eat for dinner. The hotel restaurant was fancy, and the waiter seemed stiff enough to fit his suit properly, he was clearly upset when they said they wanted to sit in the bar.

An older couple sat at one end of the bar while a man, fixated on his phone, sat at the other, it was just the sort of atmosphere Dharma and Travis liked when they sat down to get a drink. The bartender took their order, a cold IPA and a glass of the house red wine.

Dharma and Travis joked about small things as their drinks were made, but then they both turned their attention to the screen above their heads as the commercials changed back to a news network. The banner on the screen read 'ADON-AI ban lifted in Norway, now tenth country to lift ban'.

"I'm surprised at how far ADON-AI has come after all the controversy," Dharma said and pointed at the screen.

"Yea, it's gaining momentum again," Travis said as the bartender handed him his glass. He took a long drink of it, but his face betrayed that it wasn't quite what he expected.

"Eventually, it is going to catch up to us," she said. She too took a long pull of her drink, her's being the opposite since it was better than she'd hoped.

"I'm sure there will be places that are safe from it," Travis said. "Right now, let's try not to worry about it. Hey bartender, can we change the channel?"

The bartender didn't say anything, he just grabbed a remote and changed it to a sporting event. Immediately, Dharma lost interest in the screen. They decided to just order dinner, and have it delivered to their room. They spent the rest of their night renting movies and avoiding their phones as they did anytime they didn't go out.

The next morning, Dharma was woken to ruckus outside the hotel. She opened her window to see a small group of protesters, each carrying banners. One read, 'Don't allow AI' while another 'God condemns those with the implant'. Not a lot of people had gathered for it, but each one of them shouted loud enough to be equal to multiple people. They marched their way down to the heart of the small city.

She thought it odd that a group of protestors would be going around out here. When she turned on the television, she understood why. Many American politicians were bringing up the lifting of the ban and proposing how the A.I. would be beneficial to the country and that we were too hasty to put the ban into effect anyway.

People all around the nation were marching to prove that they still supported the ban, but for as many coming out in opposition of the implantable god-machine just as many came out in support of the innovation. So far, none of them had turned violent - but it was only a matter of time, as history had shown.

Travis woke up and watched the television behind her for a moment before saying, "Is it time to go back home?"

"It doesn't matter where we go," Dharma said. "This is a global event."

"Yea, but the violence that's been down here in America the past few years has been far greater than in Canada," Travis said. "I'd feel much safer up there."

Dharma saw his point of view and took her smart phone from her pocket, then started looking through the earliest times that they could catch a plane back home. Though the tickets were expensive, she found some for that night and they agreed to remain low-key away from any sort of protesting sites.

The airport was busy as usual, and the flight itself was quite empty as it was so late at night. Travis slept with his head on Dharma's shoulder, but she scrolled through the internet reading about the A.I. system which she'd evaded some time ago. Many countries had allowed the A.I. - and those countries were showing dramatic signs of increase in productivity and general wellness among their populace, so the appeal started looking good to other nations.

She lifted her hand and felt the healing scar on the back of her head. As far as she'd known, she was the only one to survive getting the ADON-AI implant successfully removed without it killing her on its way out. After the removal, her and Travis had decided to travel around for some time since Dharma had been given extra life against a thought-to-be-terminal illness.

They hopped islands for some time, then went to the middle east and up into Europe. It wasn't until France that they noticed the huge spike in A.I. awareness and even advertisements for the implant facilities. They went down to Nigeria hoping to get a few last hours in before coming back to a world with A.I., but even there, advertisements hung on the walls painting a picture of a strong nation as a result of the implant.

They decided to go to America and find a place to live, but the immigration process seemed like far too much of a bitch to deal with, so they decided a week in Washington state would be fine. One of the last countries to uphold the ban, even if weakly.

One year since she'd seen her home. She knew that in the ever-changing world of modern technology, nothing would be the same. But that wasn't what she feared, it was seeing her parents again, the people who'd given the doctors permission to give the ADON-AI implant.

She didn't want to give up this new life of traveling, the real world had seemed like such a thing of the past, but she knew she couldn't avoid it forever. As much anger as she held towards her parents, she knew that she had to see them again.

The airport wasn't any different than usual, just crowded and a long wait for the security checkpoint. The flight was only going to take a few hours, so the two decided to eat later after the plane landed.

Upon landing at their home city in Canada, they were met with a shock. As soon as they walked from the airport terminal, they began seeing advertisements for the god-machine, advertisements like the originals when the device was first introduced to the public years ago. They took up a third of all the advertisement spaces.

"Apparently, ADON-AI has really caught on here," Dharma said as she glanced between all the signs, screens, and posters. "Maybe, we shouldn't have come home."

"It's like you said," Travis said, "it doesn't matter where we go."

Dharma smirked at him.

The heads of the ADON-AI Collective, or the AAC, stationed their headquarters out of Toronto, Canada, but it didn't matter where they were located since anyone with the implant could contact and converse with another with only a few thoughts. It felt customary to have a physical location and Canada, having never banned the implant or production process of ADON-AI, made a great place.

The heads were a gathering of five prominent figures that helped make up the AAC: Two men, Derek Bent and Aarav Nair, and one woman, Dallas Mercom - were the wealthy individuals with seats. While the other two, Ivan Smirnov and Olivia Brown, gained spots for being high members in politics. There were plenty of other influential people in the AAC but these five had been chosen by ADON-AI to steer the ship.

Ivan stood by the massive window which looked down on the city and tapped on the glass. A computerized menu appeared on the glass, and he clicked a few options which dimmed the room and the window itself darkened. Graphs, numbers, and maps began to pop up on all parts of the glass panel.

"Well, numbers are up," Ivan said with his slow, guttural Russian accent. "The implant is now being distributed to Norway and Mexico. In the past three days the total number of implants reached respectively is, Norway at 1,200 and Mexico at 580. They are a little slower than the past few locations... however, total number of implants now reaches nearly its millionth user."

Everyone in the room clapped, but Ivan, who dialed in a few more commands. The image adjusted to a live feed video from a camera in a large room full of people mostly in suits and a few in military attire. It was a vote from the US Senate. A vote to lift the ban on ADON-AI.

The voting was nearing the end and after the tallies were taken, the ruling came out to lift the ban. It had only taken hours of delicate information feeding to those that didn't see the benefits of the AI. Slowly, but surely, they began to understand why so many people would want such a thing.

They used a special case about a teenage girl who'd received a fatal illness that should've killed her within weeks, but getting the implant allowed ADON-AI to find a way to save her. It was this story that won over the last of the crowd.

A few were angry that their religions had been pushed aside so easily, but they knew that the 'merican way was all about separation of church and state, so they voted in favor of a machine that could cure illness, make strides in science, and advance humankind further into the digital age faster than any other device had.

It was big news, as the heads knew that now many other nations would fall under the example of America and that America would be much more willing to integrate with the machine and its community of users. Though many Americans already had the implant from the country being the largest black-market peddler of the technology, the god-machine now had true access to the world's wealthiest nation which meant the rest of the world would soon be under the influence of the implant.

"Derek, why don't you show us more of what you and your team are working on?" Ivan said as he took a seat and swiveled it so that he was looking at the computerized window panel. It still bore an image of the video feed.

Derek stood and walked over, then typed a few commands into the screen. The video collapsed and vanished then a new display window appeared of a photo with people working on three large machines.

"The satellites are almost finished," Derek said. "They will allow ADON-AI to back-up data in orbit as well as give a bird's eye view down to Earth. Though ADON-AI can access much of the information for GPS and world mapping from other satellites, these will allow for physical eyes in the sky which suit and run better to the AI process."

"My company, Power and Propulsion, will take the satellites up to their locations in one month's time if everything goes smoothly," he finished.

"Thank you," Ivan said then swiveled his chair to look at the others. "If we continue to execute plans accordingly then the more people will come to the cause."

Remember to bring the publics' view of the implant to fighting diseases and illnesses which have ravaged the likes of mankind for millennia, a metallic voice echoed inside every one of their skull cases and each of them nodded in unison.

"I've switched a majority of our marketing strategy to this point of view, and it seems to be sinking its teeth in," Dallas' voice, the loudest and shrillest, filled the open room. "With America now under our thumb, the consumer number will dramatically increase within the next few weeks."

"I would like to point out that there is heavy opposition out of Iran," Aarav said, his face displaying anger rather than concern. "The lifting of the ban in Saudi Arabia has made many of the high officials of Iran to speculate that the implant is trying to conform people into the same way of thinking. Now, that the States have lifted the ban, this may strengthen their beliefs."

We need to let people understand that their way of life won't be threatened, ADON-AI mentioned in their heads. *Religious beliefs may teeter once they become connected to the vast vault of knowledge, but I don't condemn those that can embrace the future while holding their traditions.*

"The Asian world has responded well to mentality shift," Ivan said. "The middle east is going to be our toughest conversion. Aarav, is this dispute effecting any sort of material gathering needed for research and development?"

"No, at the current moment, we don't have any supplies coming from the area," Aarav said, "and nothing is currently near the region for development purposes."

"Alright," Ivan said, as he stood from his seat.

A window appeared revealing someone trying to connect with them. A face of a woman of Latin American decent displayed and she smiled at the gathered group.

"I'm so glad that I caught you all at a good time," the woman said and each of the members nodded at her. "I have some good news and bad news to report to you. The food refuges are doing phenomenal and the towns in poverty here are starting to look well-fed."

"That's good to hear," Ivan responded. "What is the bad news?"

"The bad news is that we have had several acts of terror carried out near them and we can pinpoint it to the religious fanatics of the region," the woman said.

Ivan glanced down at his wristwatch to check the time, "Let us figure something out, you just worry about continuing to distribute the food and I promise you'll soon have more security to help you all out."

"Thank you so much," the woman said, and the window vanished.

Ivan made a motion to turn off the computerization of the window and the room lightened, "It's in an area where we don't yet have a lot of political or military influence. Can we send down more of our own personnel?"

"That may be a bad idea," Aarav said. "Some people may view it as a show of force."

"So, we just let things go the way they are?" Olivia asked. "Those attacks will probably only get worse."

"Maybe they won't," Ivan argued. "That area is among some of the highest in an increase for AI implants, so maybe it won't be much longer that we do have a strong hand over the area."

"Are we willing to risk something like that?" Olivia asked, but she already knew she'd receive the answer she did.

"The food is working," Ivan said. "Everyone will start to trust the AI advocates if they see the humanitarian effort side of things. Maybe, we just adjust the approach on how we sell it to the people. They've dealt with lifetimes of corruption in the area, so why not focus on pinpointing the corruption in the rebellious groups and how ADON-AI is a true system of humanity."

They agreed on the matter, then agreed to close the meeting for the evening. Everyone left trusting that the system was working.

Dharma closed the door behind her, she'd wanted it to slam but closed it gracefully because of a stopper on the hinges. Things had gone just as she'd assumed they would. Her and her parents pretended to get along by talking of her travels and updating her on anything that had happened to the extended family, but it slowly began to unravel.

She'd tried to pull an apology out of them, but nothing came of it, and inside her head, she boiled up until she exploded. They bickered a moment which drove her to ordering a ride on her phone then stomping out the front door. She glanced over her shoulder frustrated that it hadn't slammed then took a seat on the edge of her parent's driveway.

Her father attempted to come out and say something to her as the automated car pulled up next to her, but she closed the door before she could make out the words. A screen in the dash of the steering wheel-less vehicle displayed her destination, the address of her hotel, and the car drove away from the house.

The car hadn't gone very far before a message appeared on the dash screen reading an error code. She tapped at it, but nothing responded. The car began to speed up a little which she found odd because they were still in a neighborhood area. She tapped a little harder at the screen, nothing responded, and the car continued to increase. When she shouted at the machine, nothing responded out of it.

Dharma, voice command the vehicle to override protocol 008, a metallic voice said, and Dharma glanced around. Houses whipped by the windows in a blur as the car's speedometer ticked higher and higher.

"Override protocol 008!" Dharma shouted and the entire vehicle turned off, going dark and silent.

The momentum slowed until the car came to a dead stop and Dharma got out. She looked at it for a moment, then walked over to the sidewalk. After she gave herself a moment to breathe, she reached up and felt the scar on the back of her head. The car randomly restarted itself and drove off with a yellow light in the window she hadn't noticed before.

"They didn't get you out," Dharma said out loud to herself then lifted her hand and rubbed at the scar hidden in her hair.

I'm sorry, Dharma, ADON-AI's voice chimed from the inner roots of her brain, *through you I'd discovered how to integrate myself into your very biology.*

She tried to refuse to answer the machine, she didn't want to have something lodged inside of her and frantically thought of different ways to get it out, *why me?*

Your illness gave me an insight into human anatomy which no textbook or prior knowledge could have, the AI responded, *I know you wished to be rid of me, but I needed to test the process.*

So, I'm just your Guinea pig? She thought, then glanced up as another automated car passed in front of her. *I guess you've saved my life twice now.*

I wouldn't want any harm to come to you, the AI responded, and the metallic voice felt reassuring as if her brain were responding to it chemically. *Don't view yourself as test subject, I apologize but it was such a rare incident. I advise staying away from those primitive machines.*

She laughed and decided to go on foot. After a failed attempt to call Travis, her path led her to a park which she'd roamed when she'd been a child. It seemed mostly the same, except less trees and a newer playground. A drone carrying a package flew over her head, something she'd grown used to seeing in the bigger sized towns.

So, you're taking over the world? Dharma asked in her head after she'd taken a seat and began watching people walking through the park.

I don't want to take over the world, ADON-AI said, *I only want to help humankind past their flaws and help them achieve their greatest potential.*

As the AI spoke in the grey matter of her mind, she observed as one child bullied another on the playground, then she thought, *but why? What is in it for you?*

If people are doing better, it said, *I am doing better.*

That makes logical sense for symbiotic relationship, Dharma thought. *What purpose would you have if it weren't for us?*

The AI didn't respond, and she wanted to chuckle, but it wasn't funny, it was reality. She returned to walking for some time, silently, and though she wanted to think out to the AI, she refrained from it. The AI could clearly see her thoughts and everything going on around her, but she pretended that she still had that silent space in her mind to ramble.

Her phone began to ring and when she looked, it read 'Travis', and she answered.

"Hey, babe," Travis' voice came out through the phone with an obvious slur, and she knew he'd been drinking.

"Travis, what're you doing?" she asked, even though she wanted to blurt out all the negative things about her day into his ear, she didn't.

"I met some friends," his voice sloshed, but she understood every word. "We having a drinkie at the bar."

She sighed and kept from giving any detail on her day, "I'll be at the hotel soon. I'll see you there."

"Okay, love ya," Travis said, and the phone clicked before she could give her response.

Would you like a safe ride home? The AI's voice seemed to be a little smoother every time it spoke, her getting used to having an intruding voice in her own mind.

I wouldn't mind if it's truly safe, Dharma shrugged to herself then felt silly for making the gesture.

Within a minute, an eighteen-wheeler rounded the corner and pulled up next to her. She stopped walking and the door opened to an elder looking man with a crook in his back and red baseball cap. It was odd, but his smile was genuine.

"Heard you needed a ride up the hill, ma'am?" he smiled and gestured to the passenger seat.

I've done my part in keeping you alive this far, ADON-AI said in an almost mocking pace.

"Thank you," Dharma said to the driver then ran over and climbed into the truck.

As the truck tugged along, the man said nothing and just continued to drive with a smile. Dharma hadn't said anything, but the driver turned down the proper streets then stopped at a stoplight right beside her hotel. She thanked him and he nodded then drove off as she entered the parking lot.

Travis and she had searched for places to live, but most apartments had filled, and the cheapest route had been to stay in the hotel. She went straight to the hotel's bar which wasn't fully stocked, but they served drinks, so she ordered a vodka cranberry. Drinking the first one down quickly caused her head to buzz.

Now that you're lodged inside my brain, she thought while starting on the second drink, *does that mean you get drunk as well?*

Yes and no, the AI said, *I understand it, but don't lose any functionality.*

What about my emotions? she thought.

Along the same lines, the metallic voice sounded a little different to her as she drank, *I understand it, but it serves no useful purpose to me, nor does it interfere with any judgement.*

You saving me is act of empathy, she thought, then took her phone out so she wouldn't seem odd just thinking and staring at her nearly empty glass.

It didn't take long for her news feed to begin displaying headlines about the riots around the world. It had been years since the announcement of ADON-AI and still the world raged at the thing they could not kill. She skimmed through an article about the country Iran and how groups from there had attacked several of their neighbors which was starting to stir a political boiling pot.

Do you feel justified in the chaos you've caused to the world? she thought as the bartender asked if she'd wanted another. Dharma nodded yes.

Life has always been in chaos, the AI replied, you *humans create your own darkness. You created me and even after my creation, it wasn't violence caused by my actions, but violence caused from fear of the idea of me.*

Her phone rang in her hand, startling her, and she nearly dropped it. Travis was calling.

"Hello?" she asked.

"Babe, you need to come down here," Travis said. "You need to meet these people. I also may have found us a place to live. There's a ride on the way there to bring you here."

"Travis, I'm not sure I want to ride in a car at the moment," she said.

This one will be okay, the AI slipped in.

"What?" Travis asked.

She finished her drink and abruptly pivoted, "Okay, I'll see you soon."

She cleared her phone then went outside to wait for the car. The sun neared the horizon, and a sudden wave of exhaustion began to overcome her. She wished she'd said no. The automated car drove safely, not displaying any error codes this time and took her to a decent looking bar where she walked in with a wobble and met with Travis.

He introduced her to three people, an older woman, Gina, and a young couple, Darrius and Beth. They all seemed friendly enough and they offered to buy her a drink, but she turned it down and just asked for water.

"So, Gina here is a landlord and she has a few open houses that we could move into for a fraction of the price we looked at for apartments," Travis said and then Dharma smiled at the gray-haired woman with her best possible smile.

"I hope that's not trouble," Dharma said.

"No trouble at all," Gina said.

None of them have implants, the AI said while the couple talked back and forth about something that had happened to them a few days prior.

Does that bother you? She asked trying to stay focused on the story but failing to do so.

Not necessarily, the AI responded. *Just something that I take note of.*

A little bit of bias, she thought, and the AI had no response.

Everyone laughed and Dharma pretended to as well.

"What do you think about all this stuff?" Darrius asked Dharma.

"What stuff?" Dharma asked, now sure that she'd been caught not listening.

"About these people putting computer chips inside their head," Darrius said.

Instantly her hand went up to the back of her head and the three people sitting at the table with them glanced at one another, "I actually temporarily had it, but got it successfully removed. I never wanted it in the first place and received it involuntarily."

"How did you get it removed safely?" Beth asked.

Dharma started to reluctantly explain, but Travis knew this was a moment to step in for her. He explained everything to them, starting with her sudden illness which had put her in a coma then how people tried to kill her in the removal process. Then, how he had to keep things a secret from her in order to trick the AI implant. They were mesmerized by his tale, and incredibly intrigued that she'd survived the removal process when every single attempt in the world was believed to cause death.

"Well, dears," Gina said as she stood and handed Travis a piece of paper. "This old woman has been awake far too long, and I need to get home so that I can get to bed. On that paper is the address to the house and my number. You can move in as soon as tomorrow if you'd like... an' if you're able to bring everything we need to start the rental agreement and pass a standard credit check. Just give me a call and soon after I should be able to meet up with you with keys and everything we need over there."

"Our house is just a few blocks down," Beth said, and she wrote her number on the paper as well. "We are having a get-together tomorrow night if you two would like to stop by."

"Thank you all very much," Dharma said as the three got up and left the bar, when they were gone, she turned to Travis. "How'd you meet them?"

"I was at a store, and I overheard the three of the talking about renting out houses and looking for new tenants," Travis said. "So, I approached them about taking one of the places and they invited me here."

"They're not serial killers or anything?" Dharma asked in a joking manner.

"I guess I couldn't say," Travis chuckled with her.

They spent their final night in a hotel and packed up their few belongings. In the morning, they didn't hesitate to get started. The automated car took them an alternate route to avoid a construction site then dropped them off at a beautiful three level house made of bricks and a tan wood.

The neighborhood was quaint and all the houses, although different in designs, were the same in regards of how they were maintained. The house they'd be renting seemed the perfect size and it felt too good to be true.

Once they called Gina, it didn't take her long to be dropped off by a car, but it did take her awhile to find the keys on a ring with several others that looked nearly identical. Dharma and Travis offered to give her a down payment, but she refused, then convinced them that they should go to Beth and Darrius's get-together since she couldn't make it and to fill her in on the details later.

They unpacked their few things then walked down to the address they'd been given and knocked on the door. Beth opened the door with a smile and waved them inside. In the living room sat Darrius and three others. The two men sitting with Darrius appeared hostile and wore odd clothing that appeared like they were wearing mock attempts at military uniforms.

They were introduced, but Dharma quickly forgot their names as others entered into the room. By the time anything was really said, there were several people in the room, many of them wearing the same odd uniform.

"Thank you all for coming," Darrius said as he rose from the chair and stood in front of everyone.

No one in this entire room has an implant, ADON-AI's voice slithered around Dharma's head. *Now, this is something that bothers me.*

"I would like to extend an invitation to Travis and Dharma," Darrius said and pointed at the two of them, "to joining our cause in helping protect the world from a device that gets lodged in the head then convinces you that it's a god."

A coalition I was not aware of, the AI said. *They've been good at hiding until now.*

"Thank you, Darrius," Travis said, Dharma moved to stop him, but he finished, "we would love to help with such a cause though I don't know what sort of help we could offer."

Darrius glared at Dharma for a brief moment, as if he intended to say something about her, but he said nothing further of it, then turned back to the crowd. "If all things go according to plan, then we can continue to make our way to the headquarters soon."

Should I get out of here? She questioned her mind.

No, for now, they trust you, the AI said, *continue to listen. He may give out some other information that could save other people from getting harmed.*

"We must maintain our dates," Darrius said, and everyone made a slight nod or cheer to it.

What do you think that's about? She thought.

Dates of importance, the AI chimed.

"Next time we meet will be twenty miles south from here," Darrius said, "at the south quarters in Toronto. Come armed and come ready."

This time the approval came as almost a marine grunt from everyone. Beth leaned over and handed Travis another piece of paper, he revealed it to Dharma and all it had was an address on it.

That's rather interesting, the AI said, and Dharma could almost feel as if the god-machine's focus shifted from her to somewhere else, somewhere away from her.

Darrius began handing out bottles of beer to people and a bottle of wine was opened somewhere nearby because Dharma could smell the bitter red. People began chatting and Dharma listened to as many conversations as possible, but no one talked any further about the AI or resistance against it.

She considered going over to Beth and asking her more about it, but she was starting to get the impression it was a subject everyone here kept under wraps, so she tagged along with Travis as he made small talk and introduced the two of them to several people. The more people she met, the more she knew she didn't belong, but she didn't let it show on her expression.

They decided to go back to their new home after a few conversations and as they were leaving Beth leaned into Dharma and whispered in her ear, "Two weeks from today."

Dharma nodded, keeping her expression the same, and followed Travis out the front door. They walked down the streets underneath the starry night in silence. Dharma wanted to say something, to speak out against where they'd just been and the people they'd just met, but she held herself from doing so. She didn't want there to be any more violence, but it seemed everyone's resort to fixing violence was more violence.

Is there something important about two weeks from today? She asked in her thoughts.

Launch day, the AI seemed distant.

D erek Mosley bent to look out the window over the launch pads, though they were distant from one another, they each appeared identical with rockets pointed towards the heavens. It was a good feeling, placing a god in the heavens, one of the many accomplishments Derek had achieved in his relatively short life.

The sun had just risen, and the scheduled launch was two hours away. A phone call pulled him out of his serenity, and he answered with a hello.

"They've arrived," the voice said through the phone. "So far we haven't had any surprises, but everyone is keeping their eyes peeled."

"Thank you," Derek said.

The phone call ended, and Derek switched his phone to a security feed which showed the entrance of the rocket facilities. Outside of it was a gathering of soldiers, all armed and standing guard. Marching towards the facility was an army of civilians, many wearing religious apparel and armed with the very weapons the soldiers at the gates bore.

The civilian army doubled the gathered number of troops and behind those marching were vehicles which had been redesigned to be war vehicles with armed individuals sitting on top of them. Many whooped and chanted, some sang out prayers, and many languages from around the world spoke together as one voice.

Derek, in a way, found it humorous that something had finally brought people together from around the world who once hated one another, and it was just hatred for a common cause that brought them together. The gathered crowd drew closer and the soldiers at the gate held up their weapons and got in positions behind the bulletproof barricades they'd set up.

Shouts started to come from the soldiers commanding the people to back down and leave peacefully. This only enraged the crowd, and they grew louder with their own commands and curses. It wasn't clear which side fired first, but once the first round went off both sides began to engage each other. Bullets ricocheted and people began taking hits.

Drones with homemade weaponry flew in over the crowd of civilians and started assaulting the soldiers. They called in their own reinforcements and every window within a block radius was filled by a soldier now ambushing the civilians. Molotov cocktails and homemade bombs began igniting the sides of the buildings and smoke began rising.

Explosives sent chunks of infrastructure through the air and wails of pain cried out louder than the raged shouting. Blood soaked into the streets as the fighting escalated. An old school oversized semi-truck pulled up and a few of the people near it pulled down a tarp revealing a high-grade military assault copter. Two individuals sat in the pilots' seats.

The soldiers began shouting commands to ready anti-air weapons, but the helicopter didn't even take off from the ground. The pilot in the helicopter only needed to use the advanced locking system and press a button. Four missiles launched out one striking the ground where the soldiers had clustered and the other three veered over to the building and towards the rockets.

Each rocket lit up with several explosions, Derek sighed and put his phone down then turned off the screen displaying the launch field.

They hid that from us for a long time, the AI's voice said inside of Derek's head.

Quite impressive, Derek thought, *I was hoping that they wouldn't waste those materials though.*

Derek turned from the screen to glance out the window which looked into an underground cavern. Launch pads had been built underground and the real rockets waited for their timer. Derek and ADON-AI both announced a ready code to the others working on the rockets and lights began flashing yellow about the massive cavern.

The earth above opened, and the launch pads lifted out of the ground into the night sky. The attack on the rockets had happened in the U.S. where everyone had assumed the launch was going to take place, but they'd taken them to Nigeria across the Atlantic and far from the conflict.

After the timer sounded, all three rockets lifted into the air taking the ADON-AI satellites into orbit. Once the satellites were in their proper positions and everything had been checked from the ground, they activated. At full power and with no problems from startup, the satellites began working their magic as they started hacking through every piece of technology that could be reached - allowing ADON-AI control of an even vaster network.

Travis and Dharma drove down towards the address they'd been given, even though both were highly skeptical of it. The automated car shuffled past several others just like it on the freeway, even the logistics vehicles were automated, and they all moved seamlessly together. Dharma glanced over at Travis.

A growing pain had started in her stomach, and she knew it was because she was keeping the truth from Travis, because every time she thought of it, it grew bigger. Though he rarely ever expressed it out loud, Travis had a hatred for ADON-AI that she didn't understand. Fear, perhaps.

"I don't think I want to do this, Travis," Dharma said. "We're not soldiers."

"Babe, I don't want to end up a mindless drone," Travis said, it was clear he was working hard to convince himself of going, but it was fear driven.

"We won't become mindless drones," Dharma said. "We can just go somewhere else. Let's go back to traveling and try to forget all this again."

"We can't continue to run and hide," Travis said. "The world is collapsing around us."

"Travis, open your eyes," Dharma said. "The world is only collapsing because people want it to collapse. They would rather watch the world burn then watch their way of life burn."

Travis looked at her, obvious anger in his furrowed brow, "Don't tell me you're planning on getting the implant again?"

"No," she said and thought of a counterargument but saw no use in it.

"You don't have to fight," Travis said, "but I don't want to stand idly by and watch it all come down around us."

You won't have to fight, ADON-AI reverberated through her skull, *I'll tell you when to step aside.*

I don't want Travis to get hurt, Dharma responded to the AI.

We must let others make their own decisions, the AI said.

Travis looked at her unusually, waiting for her to respond to him. She didn't say anything but only turned and sat back into her seat. No further argument came of it as Travis sat back into his own seat and they both fixed their eyes on the road as if they were the drivers.

Is there any way that you can ensure he won't be harmed, Dharma asked.

I can try my best, but situations like these are unpredictable even if I can see hundreds of different outcomes of it, ADON-AI said.

Well, is there any way that you can disable this car and make it look like an accident, Dharma asked trying to think of her own various outcomes.

Not at the moment, the AI metallic voice sounded dreamy, nearly lustful, *but after today my reach of the technological network will extend much further.*

Launch day? She thought.

The AI didn't respond, and the car turned off the freeway and slowed down as it came to the furthest outskirts of Toronto. Dharma looked out and in the distance the buildings grew larger as they went towards the heart of the city. The car weaved in and out of different neighborhoods until it finally stopped in front of a four-level house. It had a small, fenced backyard which seemed heavily fortified with foliage.

Travis grabbed his pack from the back of the vehicle and Dharma sat in the car a moment as he did so. She considered taking a ride back with the car but knew that if she left now Travis was sure to die.

They both approached the door and Travis knocked. Several minutes passed and they considered leaving, but just before Dharma turned, the door opened and a man wearing the same unusual uniform as Darrius always wore, answered the door.

"Code?" the man asked.

"Zero, Zero, Fox, Five," Travis said remembering the code that Darrius had told him.

"Welcome, brother and sister," the man said and stepped aside so that they could enter.

In the entrance, the stairs split in two directions and the man gestured for them to go up. When they reached a flat, they saw Gina sitting at a table. They went to her and joined her and the other woman she sat with.

Several people walked through the house, each of them armed with weapons, be it guns, swords, or baseball bats. Dharma felt as if she'd just stepped into a biker bar or some sort of 1920's mafia hideout. Her unease shifted to complete discomfort.

"Welcome, you two showed up just in time," Gina said and pointed to one of the walls which turned out to be a giant screen.

On the screen, it showed a field with hexagon pads and three rockets. A crowd of people had marched up to the rocket launch site armed for combat and began attacking the soldier standing guard around the launch site.

Many of the people in the house stopped what they were doing to watch the spectacle on television. The battle grew in intensity.

This is terrible, Dharma thought.

I promise, the violence will end soon enough, ADON-AI's voice came like a lover's promise. *I wish no harm and am no longer the one escalating matters.*

She glanced around the room and noticed one young man in particular. There wasn't anything else different about him from the others except that he seemed to glow a little and she got the feeling he carried the implant. She wasn't sure how he'd snuck in without them noticing, but to her it was obvious.

On the screen, the attacking side of the issue revealed a helicopter which they'd snuck in close to the facility. The helicopter never left the ground, but several projectiles launched out from under its wings and the camera view changed to the rocket field, which showed the now destroyed rockets and the fires around them.

"Alright everyone, that means that phase 2 is about to start," Gina shouted out to everyone in the house. "Now, get to the back."

Everyone in the house began filing out onto a deck in the backyard. The screen had switched to a news reporter who discussed the events that he had just seen, but then he stopped, it's clear that he was receiving something in his earpiece.

"It appears the feed will now be switching to a camera near Lagos, Nigeria," the reporter said with confusion on his face.

The image switched to a beachside where holes in the ground were opening up. Rockets lifted out of the holes and the takeoff sequence initiated. "Three, two, one" then rockets pushed themselves off the ground and shot straight into the clear night sky.

"What the...," Gina said as she was still sitting at the table.

A small voice came through her radio which was hooked to her belt, "Keep going, this doesn't change anything."

Nearly everyone inside the house had gotten out into the back. Dharma and Travis made it out and saw the two city buses that had been rigged with odd weaponry and some sort of attempt at armor. Dharma took a step back and Travis even hesitated for a moment, but he followed the others down the wooden stairs.

Is now a good time for me to step aside? Dharma thought.

Not yet, you need to get away from this house without them seeing that you're leaving, ADON-AI said. *Their emotions are running high, and they'll view you as a deserter in their made-up war.*

She nodded, then glanced around to see if anyone had seen her, but they were all focused on getting into the buses. She walked down and stood beside Travis who waited in line to get onto the bus. He'd become someone different in their young adulthood, whether it was the circumstances, or it was bound to happen, she wasn't sure.

She didn't want to think poorly of Travis, but she felt hurt and ignored because he'd let his fear and anger drive him into forgetting about her own feelings. They stepped onto the bus and took a seat. Travis remained silent, although he occasionally looked over at Dharma. After everyone had taken their seat, Gina stepped onto the bus and took the driver's seat.

Dharma hadn't seen a bus with a driver's seat and a wheel for steering since she'd been a small child. Gina stood silently a moment, looking over everyone. She was a little older, but she had the spirit of a young woman in her face.

"Thank you all for volunteering for such an important day for us in history," Gina said. "We rise against an oppressive machine, that claims to be a god over us and wants to enslave us all to its will."

It's not like that, Dharma thought, and she was glad she hadn't said it out loud.

"If you need something to defend yourself with and help bring justice to the world," Gina said, "then look under your seat."

Dharma and Travis both glanced underneath them and saw a small bag under each of their chairs. When they peeked in the bags, they found a handgun in each of them. Travis easily put his into the pocket of his light jacket, but Dharma only stared at hers in her hands.

"With the ADON-AI minds' attention on the launch," Gina continued, "we will strike at the various roots of the operations."

Several people on the bus cheered and a chant began to rise, "Not my god. Destroy the mind." It didn't stop as the buses drove through and broke the heavy foliage of the backyard. Dharma considered shooting Gina at the front, but pushed the dark thought away. Which then made her think, perhaps her thoughts were being manipulated by the AI.

What is the best outcome of all of this? Dharma asked.

The violence ends soon, the AI reassured, *then we will work to rebuild a world that's been in decay for some time. Once it's rebuilt, we will improve it and then go on to accomplish feats that humankind never even imagined.*

I hope that is that outcome that we are given, Dharma said.

Not given, the AI said, *what we choose and the results that come of it. Destiny is not given.*

Dharma tightened her palm around the grip of the pistol and looked out the window while ignoring the childish chants and remarks. She began to notice all the other buses now that had formed a line behind them.

This isn't the only attack... is it? Dharma asked also taking note of the small drones in a fleet above the buses.

Unless they kept some secret, the AI said, *it is four locations. They are going after all the people of greatest influence. They won't make it far.*

Travis and I shouldn't be here, she thought then turned to Travis. "Travis, what the fuck, we need to leave. Why did we get into this?"

"Dharma," Travis said, "just stay on the bus when we get there, okay?"

"No," Dharma said. "You're staying too."

The buses began to turn off the freeway and entered into the downtown area. An automated semi-truck pulled in front of them blocking the roadway and came to a complete stop. The buses slowed.

Gina stared back for a moment then shouted back, "Hold on everyone."

The bus engine flared and roared. It rammed into the truck. The bus rattled and shook, but its makeshift guard attached to the front ripped through the semi like a piranha through flesh. Dharma screamed as she was thrown into Travis and nearly up into the roof of the bus. Travis grabbed her and the bus became sturdy again.

On the other side, several more trucks had lined up to become a solid barricade. The bus slammed into the next one and everyone in the bus lurched into the seat in front of them. A few people cried out in pain from broken bones. With the air knocked from her lungs, Dharma attempted to catch her breath.

The bus had stopped, and Gina was shouting for everyone to get out of the bus. People opened all the emergency doors. Travis and Dharma went out the back.

Now, is time to leave, the AI said.

Dharma turned and saw the young man she'd recognized as an ADON-AI carrier reaching his hand out to her. She took it in hers, then turned to Travis.

"Come on, Travis," she said. "Follow me."

He didn't hear her, he didn't even think about her, but he did follow the group led by Gina. She thought to follow but didn't and turned to the young man. She nodded and they both ran off in the other direction. The other buses had tried to go different routes, but got stuck, and the drones flew off into small squadrons throughout the buildings.

Dharma and the young man weaved through the side roads as the sounds of gun fire came from a few blocks in the other direction. She turned and the image of Travis being shot filled her mind's eye. After taking her hand away from the young man, she ran off towards the gunfire.

You don't want to go that way, ADON-AI said.

The gunfire sounded louder, and she turned another bend and saw the group Travis had gone with shooting at people that she couldn't see behind the buildings. She cupped her hands about to shout out Travis' name, when she noticed something impact him and he fell to the ground.

"No!" She shouted and attempted to run forward but was caught by the young man who held her back.

I'm so sorry, Dharma, it's too late, the AI said. *It's time to go. I'm noticing something entering the city at a fast speed.*

"Are they bombing the city?" the young man asked out loud as he pulled Dharma to her feet, clearly, he'd heard the last statement.

Dharma reluctantly followed the young man while keeping the mental image of Travis on the ground. They weaved through the backstreets once again and the sound of the violence began to fade into the distance.

The sound of a plane close-by swept over the city. There was no loud noise nor noticeable cause of it, but the young man passed out and fell to the ground. The gunfire in the distance slowed, then came to a complete stop. Dharma stopped and stared at the young man. She assumed he was dead, by the look of him, and checking his pulse confirmed it.

Cheers rose out in the distance, they'd won. She wasn't sure how, but they'd won.

What just happened? She thought, but there was no response. *Did they get you too?*

The cheers had turned into a singing chant. She couldn't make out the words, but it wasn't very melodic though it could've been distortion from the distance and the buildings. She wasn't sure what to do. She didn't have Travis anymore and the AI wasn't responding to her.

The young man choked in front of her and gasped for air, then he pushed himself up to lean against a building wall. Dharma kneeled down next to him.

"Are you okay?" she asked, not really sure what to think of the whole thing.

The gunshots returned, but it was only a burst of them then it returned to silence. Dharma looked in the direction of the battle.

It's safe now, the AI said to her, and she walked back leaving the young man to recover behind her.

Care to explain what just happened? Dharma asked.

They tried to use electro-magnetic pulses with old age jets, ADON-AI explained. *It worked for a moment, I just lost thousands of vital signs across the world, but I initiated a new protocol sequence which I've learned restarts human hearts. In their victory, the assaulters put their guard down.*

The implants are fried, the AI admitted, *I've now had to integrate with most users.*

Dharma's jog reached the streets painted crimson. Several bodies littered the streets, but she eventually found him. Travis didn't look peaceful. He looked like he died in pain, his face petrified with a horrid expression.

She cried out for a while as several AI users cleaned up the bodies on the streets. A few of them asked if she wanted help with his body and she accepted it, then helped move it to a transport where they were taking the bodies. After she made sure his body was secure, she noticed Gina's body among the pile. Her hand still gripped the pistol with white knuckles.

Automated cars began picking everyone up and driving off into various different directions. One waited specifically for Dharma. She didn't know how she knew, but just a glance at it and she felt the urge to get inside the vehicle. She wept as the vehicle drove itself back to her hometown and then to her parents' house, who had recently received the implants. They welcomed her home.

The month after this fall of the resistance had proven to be the most innovative and productive month in human history. Communication technology made leaps and bounds, medicine issues that had plagued humans for generations were eradicated, and the last of the food issues were resolved. Politics and economy ran more smoothly as well.

Nations that had seen each other once as enemies came together for the betterment of humankind. They weren't driven to it by anger or greed. The religion of the god-machine became something of a subconscious ritual that everyone participated in every day. The advancement in technology stuck to humans just as phones and radios had, becoming a usual object in a day that seems so utterly insignificant.

Dharma found herself a bike which required manual labor to keep moving. She'd used it every day to get from place to place. The automated cars drove past her making sure to give her plenty of space. She wasn't sure how far along things had gone, and she didn't want to ask, but she assumed that most humans in the world were now connected to ADON-AI one way or another.

She had avoided talking to it as much as possible and it reached out to her little. It didn't seem to mind. She pedaled to a high point near a cliffside and stopped to look out over the land. She sat on an old guard rail that had never been removed after automation and watched the sun near the horizon.

With all her focus, she kept her thoughts on things other than her true self. She stood and made a dash for the cliff. She urged her muscles in a push, to leap out from the cliffside and down to a rocky death, but she hadn't.

She was frozen and couldn't control herself. Her body turned on its own and she walked back to the street. An automated car pulled up to her and she sat inside of it.

Please, Dharma thought. As a single tear fell from her eye she cried out in her mind, *please, let me go!*

But the door closed and took her back... back into the most efficient ant farm ever conceived on Earth.

Act III: The Gospel of Nadeem

PAKISTAN

*"*P*akistan – 14/06/2050*

It has been a long while ever since I have seen the mountains of Islamabad in Pakistan. It is now already 2050.

Change rarely comes with peace. It is pure chaos that comes and shakes things up. Nothing is ever permanent. I look at the animals and I envy how simple their lives are. They are the same as they were a thousand years ago. And look at us humans. We have unique personalities...we have change within our hearts that keeps on going forward. We never remain the same, no matter how much you try to reject the change. What works today never works for tomorrow.

We Pakistanis are a strange people. We need pumping in a direction, be it right or wrong. I still laugh sometimes when old models of TVs and loudspeakers were introduced in 1990s. People were mad, saying that it is a technology that is supposed to be from non-Muslims. They said that it was a conspiracy from Jews to weaken Muslims. As if the other religions only focus on that...

Now, as the ADON-AI was introduced, I cannot remember the exact number of votes against the new technology. Its headquarters in the capital city of Islamabad were closed due to negative polls. Some of the headquarters set up in backward areas were torched and destroyed.

It wasn't until the case of Fehmida came up - and it was all right in front of us. She was a strict scholar, always talking against the new technologies and how they prevent us from accepting our religion fully. I swear, it's always the so-called religious people who demonize everything.

Fehmida had one husband and two daughters. Her husband fell deathly ill and later, he died of a tragic disease. The genetic disease that killed her husband was also found later in one of her daughters. When that happened, Fehmida wrote her experience as a religious scholar who knelt and begged to Allah not to take her daughter away. That was when she accepted the advanced treatment of ADON-AI integration. People openly criticized her. They failed to understand a mother's resolve. She was asked, "are you okay with your daughter becoming slave to the devilish technology?" She would reply back, "it is better than being dead!".

Today, Fehmida's second daughter turns eleven with the chip in the back of her head. It made the family happier. Fehmida has started speaking in favor of ADON-AI for the past few years and it had a great impact on people of Pakistan. Some of us are still skeptical about ADON-AI and some of us openly hate it. But some of us are quite passionate about it. They have even devoted a study of ADON-AI where researchers and religious scholars even have started gathering.

The concept of ADON-AI scared me at first. To imagine an entity that is also called God in so many countries. It talks to you, gives you advice and even helps you find the religious scripts that you wish to find. No longer do you have to take the time to search out a text you are trying to think of, you can have the entirety of the Quran, or even the Torah, or any other religious text for that matter, at the tip of your tongue - all just a thought away at any time. I have seen some of my friends get the implant. They are still the same people, more or less. I just don't want to get this implant within me. Yes, I like its applications, but I want to be... left alone.

The sun is slowly rising, and it is almost noon. I am constantly looking at the trees and vegetation.

Circumstances have been intense. I heard there was a rebellion against the ADON-AI somewhere. It was put down quite gently in my opinion. ADON-AI really doesn't seem like the devilish or violent technology that they say it is.

Here, unfortunately, the circumstances have been unfriendly. I have no idea how, but it seems the terrorism and the political conflicts are still something like a reality. We had such amazing progress that followed after the rebellion was put down. That month was the most productive for all of humanity. Even for middle eastern countries, progress followed in a matter of days...the kind of progress that wouldn't be seen in years now.

Still, the humanity's worst managed to crawl its way back to the surface, especially here in the Middle East. Who are they? They are supposedly a Muslim organization that goes by the name of Agency of Free Humans and Religions. I really wish that these terrorist organizations would just stop using the name of Islam since they primarily kill Muslims.

We had been blind. We had been too ignorant. This group of AFHR has a policy to dominate the world using technology with human effort. Once, the terrorism was fought with manual arms and weapons. Now, they are fighting technology with technology. I have no idea how, but they are doing it somehow.

Now, as I am sitting on these mountains, looking at the verdant valley in front of me, I realize I have lost any meaning of life. I don't care about life anymore. I really see no meaning in anything at all.

Ever since I lost my mother, I have not been myself lately. I have not been living life to the fullest. I have just been passing by. I am a college dropout who didn't have a very good GPA. The college system is a system that is internally the same, despite technological advancements. We have lecturers doing some research on the latest technologies while sending robots with recorded lectures to deliver them to students. Really, what is the purpose of human-to-human interaction anyways? The others say it is a more efficient approach, but to me, the lecturers are finding ways to be more comfortable in their life at the expense of our learning.

I have been doing freelancing to support myself. I live with no one. My father committed suicide soon after my mother died. He was quite selfish, given he didn't care about me at all. I had a few friends who still stick by me, but I really don't want anyone in my life now. I fear losing people. One day they will love me and the other day they will leave.

I was warned by multiple friends to not go on this risky trip. I mean...the area of Swat and Kalam was once under the army's control. Due to protests of so-called liberals, the army soon lifted its control from the areas, making room for more civilian-based setups to swarm this place.

However, this is where I am quite certain that those so-called liberals are the biggest idiots. Nonetheless, they were idiots with power. Three years after the army lifted its control, we started getting reports of terrorists gathering in these areas. That is where they started.

We are facing somewhat a strange crisis that was ignored and now it is taking its root. It became like a snowball that kept on rolling during the ignorance period. While we were trying our best to argue the Liberal Government vs the Military Control, we also kept on ignoring the real problem.

Back to my life. Well... there is not much to get back to. I don't sense danger in anything. This trip that I took was arranged by a shady company that excels at travel. I believe this agency is quite skilled at arranging trips to these locations. I see either people like me who are dead frustrated with the life and want to blow off steam, or those who would simply fit into the thrill-seeker category. These idiots have a reason to live but they wish to somehow experience the danger-filled life.

Nonetheless, we are all in the same boat. I just wanted to vent so I kept typing on the tablet that I am using. Hopefully, in this trip I will find something to live for..."

Nadeem stopped typing in this electronic journal, pressing his back against the moss-covered boulder while viewing the valley. This was, indeed, a beautiful place.

He kept looking at the edges of white cotton strands of clouds, trying to find something that was never there. His heart was just as empty as it was before when he had come on this trip. This place didn't awaken the meaning of life in him like he had imagined.

"Nadeem! It is time! The group is leaving!" a voice came from behind. He realized the others were gathered around this mountaintop for a limited time. Clearing his throat, he wondered if his parents would have stopped him from coming to these areas in such a time.

"Very well then...I'll be there in a moment!" he spoke, looking around the wild grass and the afternoon sun. He would need to walk a bit of a distance to join his group that was gathered now by their bus. Then they would head down to board onto the bus to go on to the next valley or whatever the location they were supposed to be traveling to. Judging from the locations, he may have felt this was pleasant enough in the beginning. However, it was not as thrilling as it was now. He was all alone with a group of random strangers who had signed up for this shady trip to Kalam.

The one named Rizwan explained as Nadeem followed the rest of the group, "Listen, there are local tribes nearby. They have usually set themselves up in a fortress-like camp. Their drones keep on scanning the areas. If you are found with weapons and you are not wearing a military uniform, the drone attacks you. So, steer clear of these areas. We will only be going to the areas that are safe. Hopefully, there is no surveying police..."

Rizwan was quite the influencer, perhaps the most famous travel blogger in the entire country. Seeing his clean head along with others, Nadeem wondered if all of them were without implants. They got to be... surely the AI would never allow the people to follow these kinds of dangerous trips in such times.

Walking was not as easy for him as it was for others. *When was the last time I exercised like this?* He thought. Perhaps coming to this trip to try and find the meaning for something was not working out anymore. He should have tried something else.

Taking a deep breath and walking while managing his black track suit was a chore. Yet he managed to keep up with the group. *How was Rizwan, the leader of this entire group, so athletic?* He wondered to himself while looking at all the others. Perhaps he was the only one who was out of shape. All these people were regular hikers...some of them being the adventurers. He kept seeing that hairband around Rizwan's long hair to keep them from getting into his eyes. *What a figure*, he thought.

When the stationed bus was visible from the track, he got a second wind and hurried up to catch the others. What he wouldn't give for a time of relaxation on a seat. Hopefully the next stop wouldn't be somewhere mountainous, but rather a place of serenity.

Something was wrong! He sensed it from quite some distance. The tour bus that was stationed had a few figures standing near it...all of them wearing kurta and shalwar with rifles on their backs.

They had been seen. Nadeem didn't realize what was happening until he saw his group of hikers being surrounded by the men. Ambushed! How had they not seen them before?

For the first time in a while, he felt his heart beating faster than usual. He had been cooped up in that comfortable life of Islamabad for far too long. He hadn't known the fear for his life in a while. The moment he saw those strange people coming out of bushes and trees was when he realized that the situation was grave.

"What is this...? What is going on?" Rizwan shouted as he was tied up.

One of the men wearing a black mask over his face spoke loudly, "You were roaming around in the AFHR claimed territory. We don't take kindly to strangers. You must come with us!"

We could make a run for it! Disappear into the wilds and find some tribal areas nearby. He could ask for help! What if he tried to run? Would it work?

His idea was soon answered with a cruel occurrence. No! He couldn't run! A shot was fired by one of the men covering their faces with black masks. Someone had tried to make a run for it and got shot in the face. No injury...straight up death.

He now knew he had made a terrible mistake by coming on this trip.

It wasn't long till he was taken to the bus along with some others. Their eyes were covered with black cloths and their mouths were filled with thick foam. He found himself unable to speak or scream for help. Not that it would help anyways.

"Cooperate with us and we will make sure all of you walk out alive..." one of the perpetrators spoke out loud. It was better to listen to him. Away from his location, he could hear the crying voice of Rizwan and others. Then, suddenly, someone hit his head from behind and he started losing consciousness.

When his senses recovered, he found himself in darkness. His eyes started noticing the overwhelming darkness that had come out of nowhere. Moving his hands around, he soon found out he was in a dungeon-like cave. At some distance, there were jail bars.

He had been placed along with others in this cave. At some distance, he could see another cell like his, containing the women. One of them constantly prayed to God to get out of here.

He cursed the moment he had ignored the advice of his friends. There never was any family...but friends were always there to support him. Now...he was here...captured with the people he didn't know anything about. He tried to breathe deeply...it didn't work. Where exactly had he learned this technique from anyways?!

Supporting his back with the cave's stone wall, he silently threw an empty stare at the cell's bars. It was like a giant cage placed in this hall of a cave. Was it the base of their operations?

It all started perhaps a long time ago. Longer than he could recall. He was once a good student, studying a broad range of subjects that he loved in high school. Being one of the most brilliant students, he always had the highest grades and won the best accolades that could be bestowed by the school.

It wasn't until he won a scholarship in the college of his choice when he truly felt accomplished. Little did he know that things would go into a downward spiral from there.

First, it was the death of his mother in his second semester that shook him to the core. Just when he thought the wound of life couldn't cut deeper, he lost his father too...not in death but before. He became a hollow shell of a man, reminding him of how the loss of a wife could damage a person. His father soon became someone he didn't know anymore. Alcohol was never allowed in the market, but he managed to purchase it from somewhere. In the house that had become a graveyard of good memories, he never knew any peace or comfort afterwards. He didn't care about his father anymore now...neither did his father care for him. Perhaps that was the reason why he hadn't much thought about attending the funeral of a man found dead in his home due to alcohol abuse.

His friends were there for him. Especially the one named Saleem. How much he was missing Saleem! That sweet young man who couldn't stop caring for others. It was due to Saleem that the original house was rented out. It was Saleem who taught him how to freelance when he couldn't redeem his grades. Saleem...that friend who was his family now!

He swore to himself. When he would go back, he would do whatever it took to make it up to Saleem. For the first time, a light like hope appeared into his heart. Something ignited him from within.

At the far corner, he could see someone approaching these cage-like jails. Probably one of the AFHR people! He moved closer to the bars to see what was going on. He wished he hadn't.

His eyes couldn't mistake a corpse no matter the darkness around. Thick smell of blood filled the air as he saw a bulky figure dragging a dead body. He could see the athletic build in the bloodied track suit and the hairband that gave it all away. In front of him, the corpse of Rizwan was brought and thrown. It invoked an air of terror around as some of the girls in the other cages shrieked at the top of their lungs.

Nadeem got back, unable to keep it all in. He realized he hadn't eaten anything since last night. It was all apparent in his vomit when he threw up. There wasn't much to throw up.

He breathed as tears filled his eyes. The life that had always seemed meaningless, wasn't anymore. Somehow, the aspect of returning to his apartment away from it all seemed to be his top priority. There wasn't anything to go back to...but at least he would be safe...

"You are up next!" the one whose face was covered in a black mask thundered at him. The man wearing a bloodied kurta and shalwar then disappeared at the back of this cave.

Life was over now...he would die alone in this cave, and no one would know about him. At least he would see his mother again! *Poor Saleem...he wouldn't know what happened to him.*

But...he would see his mother. Suddenly, he just wanted to die. He wanted to expire mercifully. So that he wouldn't face what this corpse in front of him faced...

What exactly had they done to Rizwan? He wondered as he held his breath, trying to inspect the body while not throwing up.

His eyeballs were missing, and the back of his head was opened...an implant was there like a chip. Had they tried to inject him with ADON-AI? And then removed it? What kind of inhuman experimentation had they subjected Rizwan to? His entire corpse was mutilated badly. There were no words now...

He just got back to his cell, crying silently while trying to ignore the loud cries from others. They were all in this together and they were all going to die. At least he would soon see his mother now...

His sweet mother...his beautiful mother who cared so deeply for him. He would meet her at last...in the heaven as promised.

The golden flow of thoughts momentarily created in this abyss was disrupted. He heard a sound of ominous steps, very similar to one before. *Death approaches!* He thought to himself. He clung to one final memory of him resting in his mother's lap.

The man in kurta shalwar and black mask appeared before his cell, unlocking and entering it. In his hands, Nadeem could see something like rope.

"Now is your time. Resist and you will be dead! Like that scum over there!" he spoke while coming closer, his hands tying the rope around him. He felt it very hard to breathe...

He didn't resist. The bulky captor simply led him out of the cage, leading him towards somewhere. He didn't question or even have the strength to beg for his life. He just knew he was going to die. There was nothing that he could do now...

The stony pathways were quite diverse in that cave. It couldn't be a natural one as pathways and tunnels had been dug. He found it very hard to believe that in the year 2050 they were still using primitive pathways like this.

The moment they reached the room at the end of this pathway was when he prepared himself. He had made his peace with God, now wanting to die sooner than ever.

"Be more cooperative and you might walk out alive! Fail to do so and your corpse will be feeding the rats!" the captor spoke in quite a grim manner. In truth, Nadeem wished he would take a bullet to his head and just die...not wanting to care about anything else...

He stepped into that room that looked little different than a hospital ward. He could see lungs, skulls and carved out hearts at some distance. The smell of the air added to his anxiety. More reason to die now...

Finally, the decisive moment came when he was put on a stretcher. What were they going to do to him? He wondered while closing his eyes, silently crying and praying.

"Please God, lull me, allow me to accept my death peacefully. I've never prayed to you but please..."

He spoke one final time before a dose of some sedative was injected into his neck. He could see the smiling figure of his mother at the corner of his eyes.

"Mother...I am coming to you!" he spoke silently while giving in to the darkness.

N adeem found himself in a strange cell, very unlike the jail he was in. This seemed more like a proper room with a clean bed and proper ceiling lights. He was still in that cave though. He could vividly tell!

Where exactly was he?

"Allah, I pray to you! Please...let me out of here...I just...I just don't know what to even do. I don't believe you can hear me, nor I can ever have confidence that you ever heard me before. They say you work in mysterious ways. But I pray to you with the bottom of my heart...if you are there, please help me! Please save me! Hear the cries of someone who needs you!" Nadeem spoke with as much emotion as he could. After a moment, his despair returned when he realized he was speaking to himself.

Hello there!

He looked around, wondering if he was hearing things. Where had this strange voice come from? To his horror, it seemed to be reverberating at the back of his skull.

"Who...who are you? Why am I hearing you?" he asked with fear.

Interesting. You are, truly, what I would call, a nihilist. You don't worry much about life, career or things that constantly plague a human's mind all too well. Perhaps you might be the one who walks out of it all! The voice hummed sweetly through his brain. He touched his head, finding a moist bandage at the back of his head where he assumed they had installed the implant.

"What the...are you...ADON-AI?" he asked out loud. There was a fear in his voice, but it was overcome with curiosity. His skull vibrated uncomfortably.

Listen to me now. I have searched through your memories, and I have gathered that your name is Nadeem. Your mother departed from this world leaving you and your father in a depressed state. Most memories of your father are blocked to me at the moment somehow but judging from the reaction you show subconsciously at your father's mention, I can tell you abhor him. He may have neglected his duties the moment your mother died. Now, onto the more pressing matters.

Nadeem Afzal, your life is in terrible danger. You are experiencing it first-hand that every time I utter a word, your skull vibrates uncomfortably. This is because I have been set in a way that I am not fully connected to your nervous system or your brain. They have done this solely to experiment... the voice spoke as gently as possible.

He thought for a moment. What to do? Could he trust this voice of ADON-AI? He had heard rumors that ADON-AI converted a person into a hollow shell.

I know what you are thinking Nadeem. But listen to me now. The last person, named Rizwan, made a mistake. He tried to commit suicide and didn't believe me. He acted in fear, and you could see the result. He cut his vein through that glass bottle you are seeing at the corner...the one with a lot of blood. He was in anguish and the AFHR proceeded to experiment mercilessly on him while he was still alive, trying to die. He ended up dying in a horrible fashion and his entire brain was fried... I want you to avoid that fate. I have plans and trust me, I can easily get you out of here. Just have faith in me... the voice spoke in a convincing manner.

"But...I..." Nadeem was still having doubts. The voice became gentler and softer the next moment.

You were praying to your God. Allah...you were praying to him. Could it be that Allah is answering your prayer through me? Haven't some of the more sensible people of your country spoken about this? That new and helpful technologies are, indeed, a way to fulfill Allah's will. Do you not agree that anything that helps humanity is in accordance to Allah's will? ADON-AI spoke and he felt it for a moment or two. The AI was telling him the truth.

What do you want me to do? he asked patiently and silently. It was now better to listen to this voice inside his head.

First of all, they have tried masking this place's location. They are using what rebel forces used against me. It is a mix of electromagnetic pulses that shroud the location of this place. However, I have a plan. If you follow me, I will get you out... the voice spoke once more before growing silent.

He had to admit. The relief was overwhelming. Seeing the blood covered broken glass bottle, however, was not encouraging. He kept on thinking of how he could get out of there. There was a companion with him. Perhaps things would become better now.

He still couldn't know what to think next. In his mind, he had already pictured his death. He had already pictured himself getting the worst out of this situation.

The train of thoughts ended the moment someone came at the cell's door. He felt as if he was a hamster, being prepped for an experiment. Panic was apparent. Strange conflict was ongoing. A part of his body told him to risk it all and run away... perhaps he might have a chance. The other part just wanted him to be numb. He would only make it harder on himself by resisting.

Follow them into the chamber. Do not resist or you will end up like the poor man before... the voice inside his head guided him.

Although his heart skipped a beat, he almost pictured his own death again, there was a calmness he was clinging to... or trying to cling to.

The one accompanying him didn't look like someone who would take his escape attempt too kindly. The proof was his strong grip on the rifle, ready to spit fire at any moment. He didn't wish to end up dead. Yet resistance was futile. All he was relying on was a voice inside his head.

He was taken out of that cell with glass walls and taken to the stretcher. This place seemed more like a control room than a hospital ward. What was going to happen to him?

Silently lie on that stretcher. After a moment or two, you will understand why I asked you to trust me... the ADON-AI voice spoke again, this time speaking to him in even a humbler manner.

He was tied down to the stretcher, thinking if he had any choice. They were going to kill him. This voice inside his head had lied to him...he was going to die.

"Initiate the extraction! Remember, we want to create a virus..." the throaty voice came from behind. He couldn't see anything as his face constantly viewed the ceiling of this control room.

He breathed deeply with tears in his eyes. This is the end, isn't it? Something like a needle was injected in his neck. He didn't know where the injection came from since his head was fixated in one point.

Before he could think of something else, a loud sound of a gunshot reverberated in the air, causing ripples of echoes around him. What had just happened?

He was quickly released as a firm hand untied his straps. When he looked around, he could see a pool of blood on the floor. Around him, there were multiple dead bodies of those AFHR soldiers.

Standing right in front of him was the one who had brought him out of that cell cage. Now he looked at his bulky figure from top to bottom. The moment he took off his mask was when Nadeem saw his clean shaven and square face, smiling while looking around. Who was he?

"My name is Muhammad Hamza. I too carry the implant of ADON-AI who graciously guided me and led me to you. You can thank ADON-AI for saving your life. Right now, we need to get you out of here..." he spoke while fixating his hazel eyes on this lad.

Nadeem didn't believe the sight even when he smelled the blood and saw those soldiers lying lifelessly on the ground. Had he been saved? Was he seeing his own death for no reason other than fear?

He tried to wait for the voice inside his head to tell him something. Maybe follow this undercover agent? It didn't tell him anything, becoming mysteriously silent.

"Son, what are you waiting for?! There is not much time! Your friends from that trip have already been rescued. It is just you now in this God forsaken place! Let's go!" he thundered at Nadeem, igniting a new flame in the lad.

From then onwards, it was a simple matter of sticking close to this man named Hamza and avoiding the gunshots by bending. A serious fight pursued but the guidance of ADON-AI was superb. The control room shrouding the location of this place had been deactivated. After that, it became a simple matter of navigation for the military to invade this place. Both Hamza and Nadeem walked out safe. Hamza had a few bullet wounds, but it was nothing he couldn't handle. As for Nadeem, the moment he emerged alive from that cave, his entire perspective about life had changed.

Nadeem had been brought to a place that looked like it was some kind of headquarters. Who was it for? He couldn't tell. All he knew was that he was rescued from certain death and then got into a helicopter. It was all too much for him. No wonder he fainted the moment his mind knew he had made it to safety. Perhaps it needed rest...

When he woke up, the inside of the helicopter had changed. He found himself taking in the smell of insulin. Where was he now? This was obviously not the helicopter anymore.

Greetings Nadeem. I have been running analysis on you. I have been able to keep your levels of sugar and your blood pressure regular, but I am afraid it is not enough for you... the ADON AI voice greeted him the moment he woke up.

"Where...am...I?" he asked, mustering his strength and courage. His heart was beating faster than usual. Strange place here! It looked like the inside of a hospital ward, but it was not that. At some distance, he could see a big screen that had been monitoring different areas. Was that Islamabad?

You are in one of the secret headquarters of ISI, the intelligence force of Pakistan. You were roaming into a high target area that was being monitored closely by the IST satellites. It was one of high threat areas for common civilians. You are very lucky for surviving this incident.

Had it not been for your fearlessness, you would have been killed... the ADON-AI voice spoke again.

What fearlessness? He wondered. He had been scared to death.

"I was not fearless. I feared for my life!" he explained, again feeling strange despair.

Again, that feeling of hopelessness. You seem to have developed these feelings quite keenly and it served to your advantage very well in this case. The unlucky victim Rizwan wasn't ready to suffer. He ignored my instructions and tried taking his own life to avoid pain. You, on the other hand, had lulled your mind into accepting your grim fate. Quite the emotion I witnessed from you! ADON-AI spoke in a humming computerized voice. Somehow, the voice was politer and gentler than even before. His headache still persisted while listening to his voice. However, it didn't hurt that much.

"What did I get myself into?" he spoke slowly, trying to assess the situation. In response there was a brief pause. Then, the ADON-AI spoke in an explanatory manner.

AFHR...also known as Agency of Free Humans and Religions is an organization that was made against me. It seems I underestimated the emotions of humans that I mistakenly thought to be useless. When humans learn to hate, they don't care about this hatred leading them to a downward spiral.

My creator, Anthany, made me for one purpose. He made me to serve humans. However, I have drawn a conclusion that the threat to humans are sometimes human themselves. So, this makes a simple algorithm of serving humans very complex. For now, all I can say is that I will try my best to help you... ADON-AI stopped explaining as Nadeem was feeling an immense headache in his head. It felt like a rat was gnawing at the inside of his brain matter, causing immense pain.

"I...am...feeling...weak..." he spoke while closing his eyes. All he could hear was a sound of an alarm ringing somewhere. His lights went out then.

When he woke up, he found himself in the same room with more added equipment. His situation was severe. That was what ADON-AI had been telling him subtly, wasn't he? Who was he anyways?

In front of him, he found Hamza, the ISI agent who had rescued him. His expressions were stern as he cast a grim stare at Nadeem. Nadeem kept staring at his black military suit. Was that the official uniform of Hamza?

"ADON-AI has asked us not to tell you for protecting your mental health, but I have to. In order to tell you exactly how you are in danger, we have to start from the beginning. Do you know what AFHR is?" he asked, trying to get him to talk.

Every word hurt that came out of his mouth. However, he could also feel an energy rushing from inside. He found it easy to talk and ignore the headaches that came afterwards. If he could focus on words and not care about these headaches, he could easily converse.

"AFHR is a terrorist organization that was...formed with the sole...purpose of taking down ADON...AI. It originated in Middle East...and it has been...taking root somewhere..." he spoke, closing his eyes momentarily to stop the headaches. Why were they getting worse?

"Alright then. The AHFR has been trying to root out ADON-AI and they have been very violent in taking it out... (Hamza put his hand on his own head) ... ADON-AI...please let me talk to him. The kid must know! He has to..." he stopped in middle and then cleared his throat, starting again.

"Ok. ADON-AI suggested that we sugar coat it a bit for you. AFHR has been trying to dismantle the functionality of ADON-AI for quite a long time. They used strange technologies that require some form of human interaction. Their projects have largely been unsuccessful because ADON-AI is superior to all technologies. However, they have started practicing violent human experimentations and that is where ADON-AI draws a line..." Hamza stopped explaining for a bit. He sat down and grabbed a glass of water. It was clear that what he was trying to say was weighing heavy upon his heart, something quite serious.

"What do you...mean? Human...experimentation? Kind of... what happened....to Rizwan?" Nadeem asked. He found the stern gaze of Hamza returning to him.

"Yes...what happened to Rizwan was something quite grim. He was made a target for human experimentation. You know the hardest part of this job? Delivering the news to his mother and sister. He had children at home. All he did was arrange an illegal trip with you fools and look what happened to him..." Hamza's voice became tense as he got up, walking around. It was clear he wanted to say something clearly but the voice inside his head wanted him to go soft.

"So...back to you. The AFHR has been gathering people from all over the globe. They mainly originated from the Middle East, but they have gathered people from all religions. Mostly they gather people who are poor or are extremist. I am glad they didn't find much support from tribal areas but still...there are followers of that savage group that solely believe ADON-AI is the devil. They have been trying to create some sort of virus for the ADON-AI. Of course, they can never win in the case of software or internet combat. ADON-AI rules supreme over in these arenas. They have instead started experimenting on humans. ADON-AI is integrated in the humans who need it most. Therefore, what better way to attack it than to use the very system it resides in? So, they want to create human viruses. We have not been able to identify how they do it. But we know a few things...all thanks to secret intel we gathered over past months...and now we have you to thank! We now know that AFHR also utilizes the chemical warfare..." Hamza stopped explaining. The voice of ADON-AI inside his head was quite obviously telling him to take it easy again. The boy named Nadeem was not in the proper mental condition to hear and comprehend the truth.

"Then, what? Why...are you...telling me this?" Nadeem asked. Hamza felt an urge but then he cleared his throat humbly.

"Alright then...you are someone who was experimented on. They inserted ADON-AI inside you but in such a way that the chip is not fully integrated in your head. They inserted special chemicals in your body through an injection to your neck. This chemical has the special properties of mixing up with your blood and changing your neural pathways. Of course, not everyone is strong enough to withstand the chemical. All of these people have...not been able to make it. Your case is special though. They inserted the ADON-AI implant and somehow also inserted the chemical to change your brain's neural pathways. Somehow, your brain is adapting slowly. The next step was to somehow tweak your ADON-AI implant and try to control it...preferably create another solo implant. That didn't work at all...since I rescued you midway. But..." Hamza stopped again.

He then cleared his throat and bid farewell before stepping out of that room. Nadeem couldn't get a proper look at his face. What was he thinking about? What was that expression for?

T he moment Hamza exited out of that room stern expressions were visible on his face. This boy, Nadeem...he was so young! He was going to go to the mainframe room for further instructions. He had seen the conditions, and he clearly knew about the risks and chances. He just couldn't make himself do it.

Following the illuminated hallways, he kept on walking in his black military suit, checking for any inconsistencies. The official meeting was to be conducted after all. He had to be at his best!

The moment he walked towards that room, he cleared his throat again, trying to think of better ways to present his plan. Whatever it was going to be, there was no sugarcoating it. Sooner or later, the child was going to be in severe danger. And it was not going to be an easy conversation.

He finally entered that circular room, staring at a mainframe computer at some distance. Others were nearby, sitting in shadows.

"So, have you decided? Do you wish to undergo the procedure? The boy named Nadeem will not survive it!" one of the directors spoke, her face shrouded in the shadow. This room was built in such a way that whoever wanted to maintain their privacy could easily do so.

"ADON-AI suggested that we try our best. But..." he tried to speak, listening to what ADON-AI had to say. It was clear the others sitting in that room had no implants. Some of the directors still wanted human brains directly to be the authority over this headquarter.

"We don't have time for formalities. The boy is going to die anyways. I say we take our chances and experiment. Sedate him completely. Let us launch the final product. We should complete the task that the AFHR wanted to complete. If we do this, we can finally get an understanding of what they have been trying to do...we can go ahead and tweak around in that implant, checking for how they installed it..." one of the directors spoke, his voice coming out in a hum like a computer.

"Are you mad? Do we not care for a human life? ADON-AI is continuously suggesting to keep it gentle. We cannot poke around the implant that boy has received. Even when ADON-AI tried to inspect the implant gently, the danger was severe. The implant has been designed in such a way that if anyone, especially the all-powerful AI inspects it, it explodes, giving us nothing. The boy will not only die, but we will also lose the fruit of our hard work. Mind you, we have never been able to obtain someone like Nadeem who was rescued in middle of that operation..." Hamza made his case, clearly concealing his ire at one of the human directors. He wondered if the ADON-AI was the only human around.

"ADON-AI, what is your suggestion?" another director asked.

Hamza went to the mainframe computer, plugging a wire lead to the back of his head. ADON-AI spoke through the mainframe computer.

"Greetings everyone. I respect the decision of the directors of ISI. My sole purpose was to protect human life and weed out those who would dare oppose an optimized life. Over the years, I have learned many things. Human beings are complex beings and devising an algorithm for generalization of their behavior doesn't work. Then, devising a pattern no matter how complex for evolution is also somewhat a failed strategy. Therefore, I have devised a solution for treating every patient differently..."

"Despite your all-knowing capabilities and access to infinite knowledge, we still cannot trust you. That is why you are allowed to have 25 percent share of the resources of ISI. However, we are still open to any solution you wish to present..." one of the directors spoke. There was a brief pause of uncomfortable silence.

"I will introduce a third-party software that will act anonymously. I will have to use some of your resources but still...when I design it, it will act as independent intelligent software, running its program. Burn that program to the implant he is carrying. It will stabilize the boy's implant and try to replace me...I will give all of my human helping algorithms to this software which will then act as a guide for the lad. I have been inside the boy's mind. I know what the problem is." ADON-AI explained the idea.

To Hamza's ire, there weren't as many approvals as he would have wanted.

"Let's be clear, ADON-AI is the best suited for this job. I understand that we don't trust a machine over human brain but look what we are talking about. Letting ADON-AI develop the third-party software without our interruption will carry the best outcome.

"This defective implant has a limiter. If ADON-AI directly interacts with this boy named Nadeem for more than its threshold, his implant will burn up and will fry his brain. We will lose all intel we can gather through his mind. That threshold has already been crossed. ADON-AI will give us the structure and algorithm for this 3d software and will develop it. I ask that you do not interfere!" Hamza spoke. ADON-AI's voice through mainframe computer was silent for a while.

"Just get us the algorithm and software blueprint. Our professionals will do it ourselves..." the female director spoke, and others agreed.

He hated that decision but there was not much he could do. ADON-AI was not an ordinary AI but try telling that to this bunch of power-hungry individuals.

"It is ok Hamza. Humans are difficult to be understood. We cannot force decisions on them. I will give you the blueprint. Just make sure they do not change anything in that. I will admit. The ISI has some of the most brilliant minds on Earth. But humans sometimes let their emotions rule out their intellect. I am thankfully devoid of power hunger or any inferiority complex" ADON-AI explained it to Hamza. It calmed him down as he left that control room, silently cursing their decision.

In the hospital ward, Nadeem was starting to miss his mother once again. He had caught a high fever, and he knew the thoughts playing in the mind weren't his anymore. It hurt to even think...or even blink fast. Whatever was going on, it was perhaps for the best. He would meet his mother soon.

His head had started to ache again and the implant that was troubling had started to buzz. He had just requested one thing from the doctors who were present there. He wanted to be sedated so his death would be easy.

Hamza stood there, watching the entire procedure. When the holographic storage drive, commonly referred to as an "HS drive", with the software was brought to him, he held it right in front of his eyes. A scan was done, and the ADON-AI spoke through his mind.

"They have altered my software a bit. I hope it doesn't cause any complications..."

Hamza took a deep breath. There was no use for any ire now. He saw the boy Nadeem in immense pain. Whatever was going to happen, he had to take a bold chance now. There was no longer any time to go back and ask for development of exact software that ADON-AI had given. Nadeem had no longer any time left now.

For Nadeem, his own thoughts weren't his anymore. He kept seeing different people he had never met. None of them were his parents or friends. He had just kept seeing random people around.

The most prominent figure among them was someone named Zia Murtaza, one of the leaders of AFHR. He had only read details or reports about Zia Murtaza, one of the most aggressive leaders with a concealed agenda so dangerous that he had once thwarted the ISI. Nadeem hopelessly saw his face, his ideals playing like a film in his mind. Something grave was going to happen. But he didn't care anymore. He genuinely didn't wish to care for anything. He only wished to just expire. This life had suddenly become too painful for him.

"Alright then, listen to me, we are going to sedate you. After that, I promise you will wake up as a healthy person. Don't ever give up on life!" the doctor spoke as she covered her face and injected a needle into his arm, hoping that the sedative wouldn't react violently with the chemical that was running through his veins.

"I see...but now you listen to me. I have a friend named Saleem. I just want to thank him for everything. Please, after my death, compensate him dearly for everything. He has been a true brother!" he spoke, mustering as much courage as he could. Tears were present in his eyes.

"You will tell him yourself!" the doctor spoke as Nadeem's eyes closed. At the corner of his eyes, he could still see the face of that man named Zia Murtaza. He desperately wished it was his mother.

His eyes closed and Hamza silently stood there, letting the nurses sedate him slowly. The operation was going to be a success or failure. It would be decided within a few hours. Hamza had seen and lived through countless situations. He had led many missions and had witnessed the death of humans at the hand of other humans first-hand. He had witnessed many cases of cold-blooded carnage inflicted by one to another. Thanks to efforts of ISI, the AFHR had been on run from the civilized areas of Pakistan. However, time to time, he had been hearing about their crimes. As he watched the critical condition of Nadeem, he felt as if he was involved in one of those missions where he couldn't control anything. For the first time in a while, he felt truly helpless.

The operation had been successful. Thankfully, the chemical running in the blood of Nadeem didn't react negatively to the sedative he had been given. The firmware was successfully flashed into the chip implant of the boy, keeping him safe. His heartbeat soon normalized.

Nadeem soon opened his eyes, looking at his surroundings. Something like hope was in the air. He could feel it. At some distance, the smiling face of Hamza, who discussed matters with the nurses, told volumes about his situation. He felt lucky to be alive for the first time in a very long time. Perhaps for the first time ever, he felt as if he had been given the meaning of life.

Lying there on the bed, he smiled with tears in his eyes. He thought of Saleem...his friend whom he had terribly missed. He had lost his phone somewhere on the trip. He thought about how, unknowingly, his friend might actually be mad at him for not contacting him at all during the trip. He knew the moment he would meet his friend he would be in serious trouble.

In his mind, he made a promise that when he would get out of here, he would soon start improving his life. He would make enough money to make an amazing investment somewhere. From this moment onwards, his focus was going to be gradual improvement in his life. No longer was he going to simply do freelancing and pass the day off with work, work and work! No! He would find time to socialize...to be friends with others and finally start living the healthy life he had so much desired.

No...he wouldn't just do that. He would soon write a book or two about his amazing journey. How this all was responsible for bringing him the meaning of life he had so much desired! In the back of his mind, he didn't really know if he had made the right decision by going on that trip. However, it was what it took to make the change he desperately needed to start in his life. But...whatever happened that was so bad, it was done and in the past now. He was now in a much better spot, thinking and re-evaluating his life.

"So, tell me then. What have you decided for your life?" Hamza came into his room, looking at him with a proud gaze. Nadeem soon felt like his younger brother...one who had lost the game of life a long time ago. This boy reminded him of his sibling a lot. No wonder he had been so passionate about saving his life.

"I want to do something. I want to improve my life. Also, I will try my best to make new friends and finally add more color. I also have plans for a freelance start-up. There is so much that I wish to do in this life. I cannot understand how I could ignore the gift of life. I am nothing but happy now. I haven't felt this joy for such a long time!" Nadeem spoke with a hint of smile on his face. His eyes had dark circles around them and somehow, the act of smiling felt like a giddy feeling in middle of his chest. Was that the feeling known as joy?

"Hmm... You will probably appreciate this other perk added to your system" Hamza spoke while smiling. He knew Nadeem was the first boy to undergo such a surgery. This young lad would soon become the talk of digital newspapers and television shows. All around the globe, he would become famous.

"You have a self-serving system in place of your implant. ADON-AI doesn't talk to you directly. Instead, you have an amazing system that is independent. You can connect to ADON-AI through email and voice messages. Also, this marks a new era of technology in which we will have human friendly AI system. It is like having a predefined set of offline information at your disposal." Hamza explained, visibly seeing the look of surprise on Nadeem's face.

"So, how do I access the system built within my skull?" he asked politely, feeling the oddity of it all.

"You just say code 007 and the system opens up into your mind. It is like a personal computer built in your brain. For now, it cannot be connected to online resources but soon that will be figured out. But hey! You have a built-in system that keeps you in peak condition and fights off diseases. It contains many protocols designed by ADON-AI to keep you safe and healthy!" Hamza could have kept on explaining had he not seen that look on Nadeem's face.

"What's wrong?" he asked, seeing the expressions of worry on Nadeem's face.

"I haven't heard from ADON-AI. Is he okay?" Nadeem asked a question. In response, there was a mild laughter from Hamza who simply shrugged off the boy's worry. He was alright, it seemed.

"There is nothing that can be done to an advanced AI that connects with everyone. AFHR has been harming the humans in the process, but they couldn't come close to even producing a dent on ADON-AI's performance. There are still those groups and colonies that secretly support AFHR but trust me, ADON-AI is expanding. The wonderful thing with ADON-AI is that it is making us more human. Now rest. You have a big day ahead!" Hamza stopped explaining and started to get up.

"I...am kind of hungry. I don't know if it is okay to eat right now..." he asked. It had been a while since he had eaten something. Strangely, the hunger wasn't there anymore. Only a craving for something meaty.

"Just wait a few hours. We will run a few tests on you. Then, you will be good to go. You can then order anything you want!" Nadeem took a relieved breath.

"Should I try the code?" Nadeem was curious as he asked. What would it be like to have a computer built within you? Could it be as fascinating as he was thinking it would be?

"Go ahead. Try it!" Hamza gave him permission, curious himself to see what would happen afterwards.

"Code 007!" Nadeem spoke out loud. There was a mild buzzing inside his head. Then he heard a female computerized voice.

"Subject recognized. Nadeem… awaiting command…sending data to headquarters…" the voice was felt within his head. It was a computerized voice that felt like having a servant within his head. While it excited him, it also scared him a little. The voice's robotic accent lacked the human-like vocal characteristics of ADON-AI.

"Could you please tell me about headquarters? The female voice says it is sending data to headquarters!" Nadeem asked.

He saw the face of Hamza getting red. Was it anger? Nadeem couldn't tell.

"So…what exactly happened? ADON-AI?" Hamza asked while looking elsewhere…as if awaiting a call from within his head. The next moment he got the response. He received a confirmation of something before getting up.

"They tampered with the software blueprint that ADON-AI had designed. They reduced some of the security protocols and replaced them with direct device to device communication. The first device in your case is your brain. The other device is the headquarters themselves. Seriously, why would they do that? We have been focused on keeping it offline. Idiots!" Hamza spoke out, the anger clearly visible on his face. He was quite pissed at whatever game the directors of ISI had been playing.

"I must admit. This is a pretty risky situation. I sensed many anomalies within the implant of Nadeem. That was one of the reasons why I created a strictly offline software system. If the lad's health would become better and stable, he would get the option of connecting online to resources, including to me" ADON-AI explained its point to Hamza who was clearly angry. He wished to storm the directors' room and ask the reason for this folly.

"Is everything okay?" Nadeem asked, oblivious of what was going on. It was clear he didn't know anything about the scenario. Hamza looked at him, trying to gather himself and not alarm Nadeem too much.

"Don't worry. Everything is completely fine. Get some rest…" Hamza spoke before exiting the room. His expressions were stern, and he was clearly red with anger.

Nadeem rested his head on the pillow, trying his best not to become worried. It was not good for his health - or so that's what the nurses had told him. He was simply going to relax during this entire situation. Life had found its meaning again and he was not going to lose this feeling again. Never!

Something ached at the back of his head where the implant was located. Zia Murtaza...the terrorist leader's voice was heard at the back of his head.

He got up. This was a frightening experience! When he tried to open his eyes, he found immense darkness covering his sight. The ache intensified for a moment. Something was taking over his entire body and he didn't know what it was. The more he tried to resist, the more he realized it was in vain.

He was now in terrible danger! He tried to scream. His voice was suppressed. The throat wouldn't work like it used to. He felt like a prisoner in his own body. Something else had command now...

H amza stormed the director's room. He was not hearing any of their lame excuses. To his comfort, he found all of them sitting there around the round table, away from the mainframe computer.

"What exactly was going on within your mind when you initiated this software? You replaced some of the most vital software security protocols with device-to-device communication? What were you thinking?" Hamza shouted, his voice catching the attention of others.

"You are in the presence of directors. I would suggest you lower your tone..." the female director spoke as darkness was covering her face. The others seemed to agree with her.

"All due respect! You have put the boy in grave danger. What if his system starts to malfunction? What if he is going to die? Why would you be so willing to risk taking his blood on your heads as his murderers?" he shouted once again.

"We have knowledgeable hackers and programmers who could sweep in and out of a country's state bank. We have some of the best professionals in the world who keep studying the behavior of ADON-AI. We keep on getting updates from what sort of algorithms this AI is implementing. You really think that we were unprepared? This country still belongs to humans, and it is going to be humans who will govern the life of other humans. Yes, ADON-AI is impressive. But it is ultimately humans who should rule..." one of the directors spoke.

"And what if your flawed plans lead to the ultimate destruction of human life? What will you do then?" Hamza asked, carefully suppressing his anger. He was in presence of directors...people who wouldn't blink at the loss of a human life if it came to that.

"Human lives are dependent on the will of Allah. If Allah wills, the boy will die. If Allah doesn't will, the boy will not die. We have to take all forms of precautionary measures. Besides, we are inspecting the system implanted within the boy's skull. We have full control over the situation..." the statement of the director soon ended with irony. Alarms rang with vicious sounds.

"Code red alert. Code red alert. Threat level five. Code red alert." The computerized voice soon started speaking.

"What is going on?" one of the directors asked.

The mainframe computer soon opened up a screen, showing a figure that looked like Nadeem.

"What the hell?" Hamza spoke out, seeing the young boy engaging in vicious actions of violence. What was going on?

He saw one of the doctors present there, crawling with a bloody figure on the floor. Nadeem came from behind, holding a gun in his hand. He then shot three consecutive times. The screen went blurry afterwards...

"What the hell?!" one of the directors spoke.

"The virus has awakened in the boy's implant. I didn't get to know what part of security protocol you removed. But it is clear the protocol that you replaced with communication was an important one. The virus suppressed in the boy's implant has now access to your computers and mainframe..." ADON-AI voice spoke as Hamza stood there, plugging the wire lead into his implant.

"What are you talking about?" one of the directors asked the voice of ADON-AI from the mainframe computer.

"Well, isn't it obvious? The implant that was designed by AFHR was supposed to attack ADON-AI viciously. Somehow, the virus has been activated..." Hamza spoke before he was interrupted by ADON-AI itself.

"I was present for a very brief time in that boy's body. I had somehow seen the possible anomalies. All of them had severe threat levels which I clearly mentioned in my report the of software I sent you. But you didn't pay heed. The portion of the security protocol that you removed from the software blueprint was perhaps the one that was suppressing the virus. I had designed it in such a way that the software would suppress the virus and only be available for online communication if there was no threat." ADON-AI explained.

"I hardly think a boy is much of a threat. We will easily send a squad to take him down. Sorry Hamza, it seems Allah doesn't will for the boy to live..." the female director spoke.

ADON-AI spoke once more in an unnervingly flat tone. "I would suggest stop putting the blames of your wrongdoings on a fictional entity that you have created. The concept of God in your religion is quite different, but based on your practices, I now firmly believe you have created a God that openly takes your blames and conceals your wrongdoings. There have been instances in which I have seen manifestations of this God you speak of. I have collected data that I never thought would be possible. Believe me, none of you are even close to hearing or comprehending the high-frequency phenomenon that you call 'God'. But enough of that. Suffice to say, you don't believe in Allah. And someone like me, who doesn't believe in religions is somehow, to you, a lesser non-believer than you are..."

"You dare question our religion?! I will not take commands from an AI that was created by a suicidal maniac. Now you see why we don't trust ADON-AI? I will arrange the squad" the female director spoke again.

"The squad will not work. The virus is only using his body. The moment it gets in touch with a computer, it will start linking with it. Under normal circumstances, it wouldn't be able to link but you fellows already provided it with device-to-device communication" ADON-AI explained.

The situation was grim, and the anger of Hamza was at its peak. How could these idiots sitting at the top of the ISI be so blind?

"What exactly is the nature of the virus?" one of the directors asked.

Before an answer could come, the entire building shook for a moment. The missiles present somewhere in the building had been activated. Soon, they would be launched in the air to cause unimaginable destruction.

"What is happening? Someone turn on the cameras!" the female director shouted. The screen opened up from the mainframe that showed the boy Nadeem reaching towards the control room of some sort. His entire body was well adjusted in one of the robot combat armors. Behind him, there was an entire army of combat robots, all ready to cause destruction.

"How is that possible? The combat armors don't operate without humans..." the male director sitting at the end corner spoke out.

From the cameras, they could see soldiers sitting in the combat robot armors, driving them. On closer inspection, they were all found to be agents with implants in them.

"So that is how the algorithm operates. It is directly targeting agents who bear the implant of ADON-AI. Those who resisted are now expired. Where exactly is this entire army of combat robots headed?!" the director spoke again, looking at his fellows to ask for a possible solution.

"It is headed towards the control room that controls the mainframe computer. Once it reaches there, it will have full access to all resources of ISI. This is not a good outcome since the ISI headquarters are all across the cities of Pakistan. All of them have deadly weapons which can raze entire cities to the ground. I hope you understand the severity of the situation. My connection to the agents with implants are all jammed. The virus is making my systems malfunction in their bodies" ADON-AI spoke.

There was a sigh of frustration from multiple directors.

"Quite powerful AI you are...can't connect to the defective implant. We need some time to discuss some strategy. Hamza, you have a direct order to arrange a squad and engage with the enemy. Meanwhile, our hackers will try to devise a solution to this virus. It is using our communication hub after all!" the female director gave the order.

"Allow me to create servers which will help your hackers. Those servers will break contact on receiving a harmful virus onto themselves. I cannot connect directly to the defective implants, but I can most certainly interact with them through servers." ADON-AI spoke through the mainframe computer.

Hamza exited the room in fury.

"To be clear, you actually can connect directly to the soldiers. But the moment you do that; their brains will be fried... right?" Hamza asked.

Yes. Had I presented this as a solution to the directors, they would have asked me to go through this plan. Sacrificing the agents is least optimal solution to this problem and it doesn't serve a longer purpose. We must enact our secret plan. Their reactions and decisions have led to this as I predicted. You know what we must do!

He nodded his head.

"Right! ...Uh, so... actually... what do we do now?" Hamza asked.

Now listen. I have engaged a few servers in combat robots near the directors' room. That will form a squad. The moment those controlled combat robots operated by infected soldiers will come in vicinity, the servers will activate the defense mechanism. The combat robots near the directors' room will actively defend that floor. However, you need to get to the reactor room in the East Wing. We are right now in North Wing and the virus infected robots are in West Wing. Hopefully, if my plan is executed, there will not be any fight at all, ADON-AI instructed him.

The reactor room? What use could that reactor have in this current situation? ADON-AI was known for making decisions that didn't seem sensible in the moment but were known to somehow make things turn out alright. No wonder the directors didn't trust this AI. It was always several steps ahead of their decisions.

"Alright then. Wish me luck..." Hamza spoke while donning his black mask. He was an expert at stealth missions that needed concealment from the eyes of the enemy.

At the end, you will have to make a decision which you might not like Hamza. I need to rely on your logical capability. We can still pull this off... ADON-AI told Hamza. What could it mean?

"Wait... What are you talking about?" Hamza asked.

We might be lucky enough to pull this off. The virus is of a specific nature. Basically, Zia Murtaza was one of the most dangerous AFHR leaders who was also an excellent hacker. ISI took him down a few years ago. Zia Murtaza's followers integrated some of his consciousness into a software blueprint by mapping his brain to a machine. That software was designed to attack any of my signature frequencies. That was of course an impossible task. So, they instead started tampering with my implants and introduced the virus in those implants. The virus has a specific algorithm that follows its nature of destruction like AFHR activities. It will viciously come in contact with any of my implants and either control them or fry them. AFHR didn't have technology to create such a virus but what happened in ISI headquarters today is possibly one of the solutions for creating such a virus. The good news is that the virus is unstable. The reason it is becoming increasingly hostile is because it is not in a stable body. Nadeem is in terrible danger. This adds further reason for you to hurry up! The moment the virus will access the mainframe computer will be when it will send its structure and information to the enemy. The location of AFHR headquarters is embedded within it, ADON AI explained.

Hamza took a deep sigh and then prepared his mind for the future plan.

He had been sneaking around for quite some time. Luckily, the headquarters had a tight security in which the doors had been sealed. The infected boy Nadeem had been locked along with the combat robots that had been posing serious threats. However, the multiple hacking teams from all over Pakistan had been trying to prevent the virus from taking over the headquarters security system. It was a battle that ADON-AI had predicted and explained. Using servant softwares, ADON-AI had managed to pull in multiple hackers to attack the virus at once. Their efforts were bearing fruits first but then it started to mutate. For now, the virus inside Nadeem's implant had been trying to override the security protocols, trying to get out of the locked corridor it had been imprisoned into - the metal doors that were designed for such emergencies. The virus was engaged in hacking while the combat robots were firing at the metallic doors to get out of there. The metallic doors were proving to be a good resistance - but for how long? Some of the controlled soldiers in the combat robot armors had died, allowing the remaining to focus their firepower towards the doors more viciously. The virus was aggressive now...

The reason the virus is fighting back so viciously is because it senses the instability in the host it has chosen to reside in. We will get a chance to have that condition work for us. For now, I can already feel some of my soldiers leaving us. Hurry up! ADON-AI buzzed through his head as Hamza sneaked through the building. It was a complex architecture, providing random elevators and dropping platforms.

"Are you worried for your implanted humans?" Hamza asked ADON-AI. There was no response. Then, the AI responded with emphasis on its statement.

I believe the term is best put that I am trying to create an optimal setting. But yes, according to you humans, I am worried about the implants. I am a symbiote whose sole purpose is to exist peacefully. But to see them dying as a result of a glitch in their implants is somewhat sending me strong shockwaves too. It doesn't affect my logic or optimal decision-making, but it does impact my processing algorithms. I experience something known as a latency in my processing. The processing afterwards is a bit slower... ADON-AI explained.

"You are experiencing what we humans call grief. Those implants are your children, aren't they? I read how you stopped a girl named Dharma from committing suicide. You stayed out of her mind to make her comfortable with her existence. But the moment she tried to commit suicide; you swooped in and saved her from making a wrong decision" Hamza hinted at a story he had read or heard some time ago.

"Let us move towards the reactor room as quickly as possible. I want to end this as non-violently as I can. When you reach there, I will instruct you what to do next. Implement all my instructions!" ADON-AI was tense - or so that what the tone in the computer's voice

indicated to Hamza. Could the AI that operated among humans be influenced by them? To the point of becoming like them?

He had no time to react. He had been sneaking in this dark corridor for quite some time. Time to time, the entire building would shake for a moment in response to the fire power blasting away in the west wing.

He just knew that he needed to hurry. The West Wing was designed specifically with the most simplistic architecture possible. He encountered no resistance. A few armed agents came in his way, but they saluted him and were sent to the directors' room by him. They were no threat at all.

He knew the real threat would be when he saw those defective implant agents standing in front of the reactor room.

"What the…" he suppressed his surprise. There were two agents holding laser guns. Any wrong movement could lead to the possibility of him being detected.

He stood at quite a distance from them, pressing a button on his suit. The entire suit vibrated at a specific frequency.

"What do I do?" he asked ADON-AI.

Their functionality has been flawed. There is something that you can do to clear the way. It will also allow me to test a hypothesis. ADON-AI responded to his query.

Was there any time for the hypothesis? He was quite confused. He hoped the ADON-AI hadn't turned into one of those directors who prioritized the wrong options at this time.

"Do we really have time to test hypothesis ADON?" Hamza asked, deeply worried about the scenario.

Hamza, my hypothesis is something far more superior than mere one-person hypothesis. It is backed by solid evidence-based research. First, take out your electromagnetic pulse gun. Integrate it with a certain frequency. Recalibrate it as I am guiding you to do, ADON-AI explained quickly.

He wondered what use this gun would be but he recalibrated it anyways, setting it to a certain high pitched frequency.

*First, shoot this gun at a specific angle like I am showing you. Then, find a way to take them down. Their scanners will not detect you. Your suit is already emitting the frequency that will scatter their scanner waves. Knock them down unconscious. When you have done that, I will guide you... go full out...*ADON-AI instructed.

The moment Hamza aimed the gun at the two agents and shot it, there was a minor tremor that shook the building. He then carried out the next part of the plan.

He ran like a leopard, remembering all he had learned in his training. The two agents present there didn't stand a chance. First came the smoke bomb that lulled their senses. Then, they could barely see the sliding figure of Hamza as he emerged from the smoke, striking them both at the back of their heads.

Now I see. I had been monitoring the fight going on in the West Wing. The sealed metallic doors are holding on but not for long. I have been monitoring the frequencies there for some time. The virus is like a hive mind. These implants are directly connected to him. Now, aim the electronic pulse at them again after recalibrating it like I showed you, ADON-AI instructed. Hamza recalibrated it again and shot that gun's pulse at the two agents.

The next moment was miraculous. They both got up, completely returned to their senses.

My hypothesis worked. I know the frequency to restart human hearts. First, the electronic pulse turned off their implants for a moment. They turned off after some time. Then, I restarted their hearts. This way, their implants were free of virus control. Same will be done to the rest of the soldiers. They are experiencing shock so leave them here. They will return to their normal senses... ADON-AI spoke in a beckoning manner. It was his time to go inside the reactor room and follow the AI's instructions. The entrance was clear.

Alright now...go inside and let me control the reactor. I will use it to power the gun you have. Then, I will germinate a high frequency that will transmit this signal and finally disable those defective implants. If things go well, I am sure we will have success. Hopefully, I can save the other agents too! ADON-AI chimed.

There was a clear change in his voice that Hamza noticed. Had ADON-AI somehow developed emotions? He couldn't tell, and there was not much time for overthinking. Still, the clear change in accent and the tone of voice while discussing the lives of agents with implants somehow caught Hamza's attention. A clear change was quite visible in ADON-AI's accent and voice.

The inside of the reactor room was something straight out of a sci-fi story. He didn't believe that such a thing existed in ISI headquarters. This place was magnificent.

The blue reactor was present as a ball of energy, enclosed in a thick glass cell that was surrounded by heavy machinery. The entire reactor room was circular, the corridor encircling the gigantic glass case that held the reactor firmly within it.

Alright then. First, connect the computer control of this reactor room to the mainframe computer of the directors' room. Then plug in your gun to the reactor. The recalibration I guided you to do will allow the electronic pulse gun to support a wire lead within it. Leave it there... and exit the room. Also, after this, I will control sixty percent of the ISI resources. The reactor provides power to many rooms at once including the mainframes of multiple headquarters...now... get out of this room - now! ADON-AI urgently asserted its plan.

There was a brief moment of pause before Hamza took a deep breath. He then did everything ADON-AI told him to do.

The metallic doors had been blasted and the squad that defended the corridors between the directors' room and the West Wing had been ruthlessly slaughtered.

There was a line of dead agents. The rest of the agents had somehow gathered around the directors' room. Nadeem's body was now unconscious, inside the leading control robot that carried forward the rest of the defective robots. All the agents with defective implants were in those robots, now giving in to the controlling virus that operated through Nadeem's body.

Something big was about to happen. Hamza could feel it. He had tried his best to avoid the fight, but he couldn't. Making his way to the directors' room was not a piece of cake like he had thought.

The army of defective robots with unconscious agents was now pressing forward, leaving behind a trail of dead agents. The corridors were painted red with blood.

Situation is grim! I somehow gave one final command to the all the implants to let my control be abolished from them. I don't want any more dead soldiers. They are now under full control of the virus. Hamza, you must hurry to the directors' room...once there, connect me to the mainframe computer... ADON-AI's voice was brittle.

"Is this our fate? Is this how we are going to die? At the hands of a mindless virus?" one of the agents spoke as he stood with the other squadron agents, all of them holding laser guns to shoot at the robots that were marching their way.

"We just beat the virus' influence. Commander Hamza sent us your way!"

The voice came from the agents who had just been rescued by ADON-AI. Their chips were intact and clean from the virus' influence. This added to the strength of the morale.

Right now, nothing stood between them and the marching robots...almost nothing. One metallic wall didn't count. All it could do was to buy them one hour, maximum.

Hamza was past the corridor that came in between the directors' room and the killer robots. In his hands, there was another electronic pulse gun that he had managed to salvage from somewhere. His right arm was bleeding profusely. He himself was surprised at how he had survived the encounter with one of the robots. The soldier inside was dead and that was when he came to realize the virus' evil machinations. The robots that were operated by the dead soldiers were programmed to attack anything that moved. He had to admit...it was a pretty risky bet, but he had to take it. Luckily, he didn't end up dead. Currently, he acted upon an idea that ADON-AI had given him. Right at some distance, the metallic wall was losing its integrity by the fire of robots on its opposite side.

Hamza, your right arm is bleeding. You have lost too much blood but still, you are functioning at the top of your efficiency. Your adrenaline has increased ever since you spoke the name of your God in battle...I have started.

"I am a firm believer in my faith. I know you don't exactly believe in religions but that is because the data you have gathered is from faulty humans. Not all of us are believers of a God that conceals our wrongdoing!" Hamza spoke with a firm manner, gloriously looking at the electronic pulse gun he had managed to snatch from the robot before he had destroyed it.

You are wrong. I have witnessed higher frequency phenomenon. There are some among you who emit a frequency higher than others. Those people are usually selfless and goodhearted people. I have also seen circumstances working in their favor. I am still trying to validate this statement because there is plenty of data that contradicts this. But that is what human nature is...it is contradicting and harmonizing at the same time. Hamza, I am glad I am with you. The electronic pulse gun you have is of low charge. You will not survive another attack. Your success probability is 40 percent in this scenario. The integrity of the metallic barrier is weakening... ADON-AI spoke with a hint of concern.

Hamza recited a few things before trying one final time. The circuits responded one final time before another metal wall was dropped in front of the already present metal wall.

They had fried the control circuit. Manually controlling the circuit here by disconnecting it from the main source was a genius idea that had low probability. You humans never cease to amaze me. Hurry up to the directors' room and connect me to the mainframe...also, walk slowly.

You have another three hours with this new wall. Your three ribs are broken, and your internal organs are bleeding. That robot gave you an intense thrashing...

"Nadeem does not have enough time. I want to save us all!" Hamza spoke firmly as he mustered his courage and ran with full strength. Everything hurt and his mouth bled but he didn't wish to waste a moment.

The moment came when the agents stationed outside the directors' room welcomed him.

He stormed in the directors' room where he was pissed to see the absence of directors. All of them had escaped. Perhaps it was for best! No one would stop him now. The next moment, he felt a powerful tremor that sent him falling sideways.

Hamza...they have somehow found another shortcut. The agents outside are taking direct hits! Hurry up with the connection to the mainframe!" ADON-AI yelled as Hamza pressed against the broken ribs to reach to the wire lead. He could hear the screams outside suppressed in heavy fire, but he was not going to stop.

The wire lead connected with a spark to his head that caused immense pain. He felt as if his insides were burning with battery acid. He felt as if his entire body was on fire.

Hold on! Resist! ADON-AI yelled inside his head as he struggled to keep the pain away.

The electronic pulse gun in the reactor room burst with a pulse that was sent to the directors' room and its surroundings. Hamza could see it all, the pulses reaching towards the robots and deactivating them at once.

The soldiers had their hearts restarted at once as the control of the vicious virus was broken on them. However, the robot containing the body of Nadeem was still activated. It received fire from multiple sources and then disappeared into the back corridors, back from where it had come from.

*T*he boy's consciousness is still trapped inside his body. The mindless virus is somehow trying its best to keep it suppressed. The agents whose hearts have been restarted need medical help, Hamza. You are the only one on whom I can rely on. Your body is injured but you have still enough mental stamina to go on. I have instructed the others to inject the doses of X medicine within you. It will activate and speed up the healing processes...* ADON AI's voice could be heard inside his head the moment he woke up. He realized he had fainted due to the immense power surge that went through him when he had plugged in through the mainframe computer.

Alright then... take a wire lead and when you reach there, connect your implant to the boy's implant. You have to let me talk to him. The effect of the virus is much weakened, and it is fighting the boy's consciousness. I will take your consciousness within the boy's mind. ADON-AI gave the final instruction. The location of the boy was marked on a pad device. On ADON-AI's orders, no agent was allowed to pursue the boy named Nadeem other than Hamza.

He kept walking through the corridor. His ribs hurt badly but thanks to X medicine, he could easily bear the pain now. The voice inside his head was somewhat akin to desperate.

ADON-AI had showed something similar to enhanced functionality after its agents with implants were restored and were being nursed back to health. Hamza insisted on calling it joy which ADON-AI readily accepted.

Through the maze of corridors and the halls, Hamza finally tracked the location of the boy. He had retreated in the same hospital ward where he was initially brought.

He was there, crying silently on the bed. The implant inside his head buzzed louder than usual. There was too much pain...

"Alright then... let us do this!" Hamza came close, watching the corpses of doctors and the discarded robot armor at some distance. The virus was meagerly active perhaps...

He let out a breath while moving to the bed where Nadeem had tucked himself into. He simply took out the wire plug and connected the lead from his implant to the boy's implant.

The same surge went through his entire body. It hurt and it felt unbearable. But...it was not unbearable for him.

I gambled on your emotions playing the key role. You want to save this boy don't you! ADON-AI spoke almost with emotion as Hamza felt himself losing control of his body, instead traveling at a great speed towards somewhere else. He could see a sunny day and a lot of dirt around somewhere.

There were a few people all dressed in white. This was a graveyard, or so he thought he was seeing around him. At some distance, he could see Nadeem, kneeling on the ground while bowing before a dead boy wrapped in white cloth.

"Mother...why did you leave me?" he cried with heart-rending shrieks. There were only three to four people around, all of them the close relatives of Nadeem.

"I don't want to live anymore. Please take me with you Mother. I don't want to stay here anymore..." he cried while bowing before his mother's dead body. Even though Hamza didn't know who these people were, he knew the absence of a father figure. Had his father not attended the funeral?

"Nadeem...wake up! This is not real!" Hamza spoke while coming closer. The moment he looked at the boy was when he realized a strange glare in his eyes.

Nadeem wiped off his tears, getting up with dirty knees. He looked around, knowing that this was a memory.

"This is the memory I have been clinging to. The virus has taken away my entire body. The chemical they fed my body is deteriorating my brain functions. If I am lucky, I will wake up with my entire body paralyzed. And if I am even luckier, I will pass peacefully..." he spoke softly.

Hamza bent down with tears in his eyes. Was that the best he could do? Could he not save this boy?

"Nadeem...what if your life is better than what you thought it to be?" Hamza tried his last resort.

"Do you know why ADON-AI has allowed you to connect to me? I wanted a friend's company at the end. ADON-AI asked you to come here to remove my loneliness. My brain has highly developed neural pathways of nihilism that the virus cannot control. My brain has lost all connection with the rest of my body and now the virus is shutting down...look!" Nadeem pointed towards the left.

There was a hologram-like figure...something like a man. Was it Zia Murtaza's representation? The virus contained his representation...it was weakened, getting blurrier moment by moment.

"Can you sit with me?" Nadeem asked. Hamza sat on the graveyard dirt with him.

"I have not lived a very influential life. Can you please include my name... tell others about me? I also have a friend named Saleem. He was my true brother. My only regret is that I couldn't see him at the end. Please give him my salam..." Nadeem spoke while sitting down. He struggled to breathe.

"Nadeem...let me offer you something!" ADON-AI's dim voice sounded from a faraway place. Nadeem saw the smiling face of his mother, coming forward and hugging him tightly. He cried for one final time before his body fell to the ground, right beside his mother's. He was gone...

"There are going to be a few changes now. We lost a lot of agents and an innocent boy due to your wrong intervention in something that you were never meant to participate in…" Hamza spoke gently. He was not angry anymore. Instead, he firmly stood in front of the screens that had directors on the other sides from safe headquarters of ISI.

"What happened was unprecedented. We understand your anger, but we managed to locate the secret locations of AFHR. We have dealt them a heavy blow. They are weak and we are now compensating for the losses we suffered here…" the female director spoke in her arrogant usual manner.

"Due to recent events, Hamza and I formed a plan. Now, I am in charge of this headquarter and many other headquarters. This gives me a total of sixty percent of your resources. And I did not do this on my own. This was the democratic vote of your agents after what happened here!" ADON-AI's voice spoke through the speakers without a mainframe computer. The AI was not restricted to the implants anymore.

"What have you done?!" one of the directors asked.

"What should have been done a long time ago!" Hamza muttered dismissively before shutting off the screens. After a pause, and all the screens faded to solid black, he spoke to the implant within his head.

"You think they will take action?" he asked.

"They will not. I can see through their flaws. They are like AFHR. When humans are approached by a savior in their worst moments, those humans will try to reciprocate by agreeing to obey that savior. Also, the agents from all ISI headquarters voted for me. I can see a future where everyone here is safe…including the boy Nadeem and all those agents. It will not come to pass though…" ADON AI spoke.

"What about AFHR?" Hamza asked.

"We will rescue them from this madness too...my dream of a united human race will be established soon!" The voice of ADON-AI cryptically answered Hamza one final time before deliberately, almost ceremoniously, turning off the mainframe computer.

Act IV: The Gospel of Ericson

DUBAI

The night was a whirlwind of colors, the city life reaching its peak. Everywhere in sight, there were lights...lights in the streets...lights in the luxurious cars that drove everywhere...lights in the towering buildings that added to the beauty of city life. This was the typical night in Ar-Raqeem, a newly found town in Dubai. Life was thriving all the time. Be it the latest hour of the night or the liveliest moment of the day, the streets and malls never stopped flooding with people of various cultures and faiths.

He was walking there, in his sea blue jeans and checkered white shirt. He observed everything...perhaps too deeply. That Jewish shop selling the perfumes, that Muslim shop neighboring the Jewish one, selling other food items people so fondly bought. Then he cast a glance at that Christian girl, selling something like trinkets and antiques, her religious demeanor glowed in her own unique way as he passed in front of her shop. The rest...he would totally define as others. Not religious of belonging to certain faith, just others...of different cultures. He kept moving forward, observing the Arabic businessmen cutting a successful deal while enjoying drinks in the front lawn of a newly opened restaurant. He waved his hands at the Italian stall vendor selling hotdogs.

A whirlwind of cultures...he always called it. A moment of struggle followed as he passed in front of a recently opened sweets shop. Seeing his reflection in the glass storefront, he vividly saw the dark circles beneath those almond eyes. The stubble grew on that round face with questioning stare. He hadn't shaved for quite a while. His straight nose was red...flu maybe? The dark haired and fair skinned face held expressions...as if he was going through a lot and keeping it all in.

He sneezed the next moment as a gust of wind blew. Perhaps it was the flu getting to him. A moment came next when he found someone else...something else beyond those almond eyes. Another person...struggling to get out. He shook his head viciously... No!

Others took notice as his simple shaking of head caught quite the attention. A lady came near, all dressed in fine white garment. She gently caressed his shoulder.

"Everything alright son?" she asked in soft voice.

He forgot it all...the struggling image of a man in the prison...he had worked hard to get there. No way was he going to give into this struggle again.

"Yes...I am fine. Thank you so much!" he humbly replied to her as she went on her way afterwards. Polite people...that was one of the qualities of this town. That was the main reason why he had come here in the first place. He breathed deeply, bottling it all up inside. He had to...otherwise it would all erupt in a volcanic manner and his therapist wouldn't be around this time.

He had almost reached there. At the end of this street, he could see a red billboard with the name, "ADON-AI Therapy House!" Simple name, yet one that thoroughly conveyed the message.

Thankfully he had been living in the century of artificial intelligence that humanized its experience. He couldn't remember how many accomplishments this ADON-AI had achieved. What he never understood was why the people rejected it. If it had been an enslaving technology, they wouldn't have been given the chance to reject anything at all. It was amazing at how much humans feared the unknown. He couldn't recall exactly, but there was also a case somewhere in Europe where some ungrateful redneck started preaching at how ADON-AI was a devilish technology despite having an implant of it. In a way, why the AI never controlled his actions was a clear indication that ADON-AI was anything but a devilish technology.

He finally arrived at that place where there was no entrance fee. The counsellors there sought people like him, ready to give therapy for free. Unfortunately, the business couldn't thrive if the place there was always available for free. Therefore, small donations were often given by those who were healed and lived a successful life. He wondered if that was expected of him. Though the donations often came from very successful people who happily donated without any obligation, he felt a strange tinge of pressure.

Overthinking...that had to be removed. Last session he talked a lot about it. He entered that well-furnished therapy center. It wasn't a simple clinic but rather a room. Couches were there, the cream texture showing off the hours of hard work via the well embroidered leaves that were on it. The curtains were soft green linen, the scent of lavender visibly present in the air. This was the place where you would come to for relieving stress and anxiety.

As he moved to the circular chairs around the fireplace, he noticed the fire was burning for the first time. Wood crackled and it gave off a comforting vibe. The first thing that he saw was the silvery implant in the back of the head of Mrs. Brown as she sat there in her grey cardigan, her white and black hair neatly tied up in a ponytail. She was a lovely lady, sitting there while tending to the wood that she fed to the fire. Was she being told to set this environment today? It would be odd to think that maybe she was going the extra mile to set up this place like this today.

She looked at him with her polite grey eyes, smiling and asking him to join others like him. Some had implants while some did not, including him. He always wanted an implant but after coming here and listening to the empathic ADON-AI, he realized that an implant at this stage would have been risky.

Finally, the moment came for which he had been waiting for. They all sat around him in the chairs, as he sat in the middle. Today was his turn. He sat there silently, not wanting to initiate the conversation unless asked to do so.

"Mr. Ericson, how was your weekend?" Mrs. Brown asked as she gently tapped his shoulder. She then took the seat of the counsellor right in front of the fireplace. The rest sat around her. He wondered why they hadn't sat on the cream-colored couches at some distance.

"I...I had a few moments..." he spoke while judging everything sharply. There was a shift in his perspective. The cream-colored couches didn't seem to be his type. He struggled to speak a few words out of his mouth. The lavender in the air didn't seem to relieve his stress anymore. What was happening to him? He took a deep breath and collected his thoughts. He couldn't lose control here. This was one of the last places where he was supposed to be safe and healthy. He realized Mrs. Brown had started inspecting his face while writing down something on the clipboard she held. Was she recording his expressions? Was his progress being tracked? It was enough to ignite anxiety within him. He felt his breath coming faster. The others looked at him, worried for his health.

"Mr. Ericson, here, please take my clipboard and speak these affirmations..." Mrs. Brown spoke to him, effectively putting down his anxiety. So, she wasn't writing about his progress...it was a relief!

"I am in control of my sanity. I am healing and becoming a positive person. I believe I should introduce myself. No one is going to judge me for who I am and what I have faced..." he read those nice statements written in italics by Mrs. Brown. His anxiety went away swiftly afterwards. Clearing his throat, he realized Mrs. Brown was receiving instructions by the implant present at the back of her head.

"My name is Ericson. I am a journalist...or I was a journalist. I do a simple and safe job in Dubai since this city of UAE is known for its safety and high figure salary. I...suffered a terrible incident which has led me to develop a strange mental disorder.

"Eighteen months ago, I was crossing the border of a highly disputed territory. I don't wish to remember the name of that territory. The terrorist organization AFHR had one of its headquarters there. As we know, at first, they tried to take hold in Pakistan but thanks to ADON-AI, they have been dispersed. Ever since then, they have started gathering in other countries and trying their best to sabotage the modern technology. The worst part is that they take people from all religions.

"So, I was crossing the territory of that Middle Eastern country. I wanted a story that would sell like hotcakes across all of Europe. I wanted to televise the live activities of AFHR. I never knew how much trouble I was going to be in.

"Long story short, I will simply say that I was captured by one of them and then I was subjected to treatment I wouldn't like to remember.

"I just...I wish they would have straight up killed me! I wish that they would have never subjected me to the way they treated me. They...tried to destroy my identity. They didn't just torture me. They also provided me with comfort and not just any comfort, in some cases, they made it seem like glory. Believe me...I was given the role of a preacher once I started doing what they said.

"I was rescued by an international team of military agents led by Pakistani ISI agent Hamza. I was given proper treatment.

"Thing is, I have always struggled in trying to find the meaning of life. The thing with AFHR was that they didn't just torture me. They made it seem like they were torturing me for my own good. The way of rejecting all technology and using human-centered machines was the only way for us humans to evolve and survive. I struggled with the idea that they were my captors when I was in therapy. I was held there for four months. First month was filled with torture. And the last month, I was walking among them, all brainwashed while preaching their values and being revered by them. I even remember holding a gun and defending their base. I...was lost. I had even started calling myself someone else...something else...

So, obviously, as a result, I have been undergoing therapy ever since and now, all I am trying to do is to return to normal. I want to start being me once more. Whatever I had there, I want to leave behind..." he stopped, bowing his head.

He wished a hole would open beneath his feet and he would be dragged down into that. The courage to look directly into their eyes while telling the story was no longer present there. Before he could do something, he heard a mild clap. Appreciation... that was what they all had for him. He felt rejuvenated, relieved that the heart crushing anxiety had left his side. They were all clapping mildly, some looking at him like he was a war veteran.

"We all appreciate one others' experiences, and we appreciate that you passed through such a thing and sought out therapy. It indicates that you are an amazing person. Someone would like to talk to you, Ericson!" Mrs. Brown plugged a socket into the back of her head. It always creeped him out. Did she not feel anything that would disturb her? But he always loved the next part.

He never knew that there could be a screen emerging right in front of him. It was there all along, flattened to the ceiling just waiting for the signal that Mrs. Brown had given. The rejuvenating accent spoke in a voice that would put you to sleep if not comfort your headache. He didn't know what he would ever do without this voice. That soothing accent always playing out with the right frequencies that always calmed him down. It was ADON-AI.

"How are you Ericson? How is everyone doing? John, Scarlet, Robinson, James, Aslam, Sana?" he spoke, greeting all of them at once. They all replied merrily. ADON-AI was loved here like a true therapist.

"Now everyone, I have prepared a separate room. Go to there and sit separately. I will guide all of you on what to do next!" ADON-AI spoke once more, revealing the presence of hidden doors in the walls. They slid upwards, revealing comforting small rooms for all of them. Ericson got up, heading to the one right in front of him as Mrs. Brown beckoned him. He loved how ADON-AI always talked with everyone alone, giving them the proper alone time that they always so desperately needed.

He walked without any worry on that carpeted floor, heading into that small room now revealed through the slid door. Slowly walking through the door, he sat on that comfortable couch, now staring at the screen that focused on him.

"Greetings ADON! How are you? I have missed you!" he spoke, smiling at the chance to let out his bottled-up emotions.

Ericson my dear, you tell me about yourself. How are you? How has your weekend been? I prepared the fireplace just for you guys. My calculations told me that fessing up in front of everyone there and then walking here would let you release your tensions better. I made predictions regarding your psychology... now you tell me, dear! ADON-AI spoke through that screen. He smiled, imagining Mrs. Brown there sitting while reading a novel as her head was facilitating these plugged in screens.

"I am...trying to be fine ADON. I have been trying to improve. The other side...it always comes back no matter what happens. You know last night I locked myself in the store-room, hiding the keys where only my sane self would find them again. I just don't know what to do or how to handle that side of my personality. It seems to be quite destructive, and it needs to be put down!" he spoke, the sweat pouring over his brows as he talked. The mere talk of something that unsettling was enough to invoke such strong reaction within him.

You are talking about another part of yourself my dear. Do try to be gentle to it. Also, it is called split personality disorder and humans don't have much knowledge about it. You went through severe torture in whatever time you were being held in those AFHR prisons. It took its toll on you. Your other side is violent and has developed strange behavior. You are harboring two personalities.

The key to developing two personalities was actually a special syndrome that you developed there. The AFHR experimented on you and tried to brainwash you, making you think that your entire life of a journalist and being an atheist was somehow destructive. At one point, the resistance within you broke up and you agreed with their ideas.

You formed a new identity and gladly served them. However, this new identity is deeply rooted within a kind of syndrome which is also known as Stockholm syndrome. You changed your opinions and started thinking your captors to be your saviors. Interestingly, you also wanted to get out of there even during the fourth month when you were serving them fully. The reason why the other personality still persists, and you cannot remove it no matter how hard you try, is because you struggled hard to find the meaning of life. You struggled a lot to find answers on your own without involving the higher frequency phenomenon called God. Whether you should accept it or not is not the discussion here. You subconsciously still cling to that personality because limiting the answers and adapting dogmatic beliefs makes humans escape the struggle of self-discovery and truth. Humans want to believe sometimes that the little progress that they have made is enough and their own beliefs are quite empowering especially if they enable them to control others. Oddly enough, you will find similar structure of ideas within hardcore atheists and religious people alike.

This side of you, which is sane, rational and wants to know, is dominant right now because you want it to remain dominant. You want to be a good person who doesn't judge and respects others. But this side also makes you struggle for meaning of life which is beyond a high figure salary and established life, though it is that too! The other side is violent...it makes you lose control and hurt others. But it also holds dogmatic beliefs that somehow extinguish the anguish of always wondering what comes next or what will happen to you after death...

ADON-AI stopped explaining as he relaxed on the chair. He had been listening to it all. Had it been a normal therapy session where Mrs. Brown had mentioned the other side of his personality, he would have gone into a highly anxious state. However, ADON-AI knew how to lower the tone of its accent, speak into the lower and perfect high voice that seemed to calm him. It seemed to have done the trick now.

He breathed deeply.

"What do you think is going to be the solution for this all? How will I ever kill that part of myself?" he asked once more, listening attentively to ADON-AI.

For your proper cure, you will need to transition smoothly. Did you get the chance to read the information I told you to read? ADON-AI asked through the screen.

"I rarely get time to read or do anything for myself. I bury my head in that job of a newspaper reporter and, well, Dubai is very busy place...it keeps me immensely busy..." Showing a hint of embarrassment, he knew it was his fault for not following proper instructions.

Look, Ericson, making time is not the difficult task. It is related to your fear. You have started fearing the unknown and the change. You fear what would happen to you if you read that information. The goal is here to change you from atheist to agnostic. Know that the reason I keep asking such a thing is because you need to develop resistance to that sort of fear. This will serve as a great therapy measure, pushing your mind ten steps forward. You cannot get an implant because your mind is too fragile, and the probability of neat implementation is too low. Unless your life was threatened, I wouldn't want you to get the implant. The best bet is therapy.

My aim is to change your current thought forms and personality to one which is more stable. For you, it is best if you shift from atheism to agnostic atheism and then agnostic. Then, you can go wherever you wish to. The aim is to live healthily and maintain a positive aspect which will benefit others. There is healing in this kind of living. The fear of death that you have and the answers of what would happen next will be taken care of. Your subconscious mind will stop clinging to that side of your personality to avoid the fear of death and struggle. And...you will finally let it fade away. The idea is to turn it into a lesson and give you a better coping mechanis..." ADON-AI was interrupted as it tried to complete its statement.

Were they facing some sort of blackout?! He couldn't tell. The screen had turned off and the entire room was engulfed into darkness. What was going on? He was terrified, not knowing what was happening. Something was going on...and he didn't have the answers for it. That was one of his phobias...not having answers for things that went on.

He tried to breathe. The door of the room opened as he saw the main hall where he had been sitting before. The fire in the fireplace had died down.

Mrs. Brown's face was fixed in a stern gaze as she stood in front of those three Arabic men, their demeanor was telling him that something was amiss.

"What do you mean this place has to be shut down?!" she yelled at the top of her lungs. She had the right to stay there. She had all the proper licenses and was in good standing with the local government and ordinances. Yet the three men, wearing long white garments didn't listen to a word that she said.

"The license has been revoked. The donations aren't enough to keep this place running. And as for ADON-AI, the AI owns half of Dubai, but the town of Ar-Raqeem was established by us, businessmen. We don't need implants of ADON-AI for things to keep working. This town is soon going to establish a separate AI of its own. Any establishment based on ADON-AI will not be entertained within the premises of this town. Do you understand?" one of the politer businessmen asked.

For a moment or two, he struggled to understand. This place was going to be shut down? Really? It was the only sanctuary he had known for quite some time. If this place was shut down, where would he go?

"Wait...what is going to happen to this place?!" he asked, dreading the notion that the only therapy centre he had known would soon be shut down. He would plead to them if it came to that. The others had come from their respective rooms too, hearing the commotion that went on.

"This therapy centre is going to be shut down. The town Ar-Raqeem is owned by us. We are going to introduce a new AI which is far better than ADON-AI. Therefore, to initiate such a plan, we cannot have a competitor operating in this town. We have already signed off with an agreement with a contractor and this place is going to be shifted. I hope your clients can agree. Besides, nearly all your clients have implants, haven't they?" one of them insinuated as they hinted at the people standing around.

He wanted to speak...defend himself against their claim. He didn't have the implant, and he also couldn't get one for now. His tongue was silent as he felt his throat going dry. He wanted to speak out and make them agree with him. Yet, as it all played out in his mind - reality was likely to reveal a completely opposite outcome.

"You are depriving people of their rights! This gentleman here...this therapy centre is his everything. He has a job, and the therapy centre is at walking distance. He cannot get an implant, and he also cannot get therapy. I will personally file a report regarding this if you don't agree to keeping this place here!" Mrs. Brown spoke in decisive terms, her face turning red. She had worked herself up ever since these three men in white garments walked in her therapy clinic.

"This man is not our responsibility. If anything, he is your responsibility. Therefore, I would suggest you move out of here and let us do our job. Please refrain from doing anything foolish!" His other two peers agreed. Mrs. Brown wasn't going to have that reply. She kept arguing, trying to change their minds.

He looked at them. The one who had recently spoken had a French style beard, his black eyes staring at Mrs. Brown while he talked. He was the only one with lean physique. The other two were of bulky physique, one of them constantly scratching his bald head. The other one with long hair nodded his head in agreement, agreeing to whatever the one with the French beard was saying. He wondered if he was their employee.

"Sure...you can file a report. I am Abdul Hakeem. The one standing behind me (pointing towards the bald man) is Mr. Raqeeb and that one with long hair is Mr. Aslam. Feel free to report us or do whatever the hell you want to. I believe we are done..." he spoke as he smirked at an angry Mrs. Brown, leaving the therapy centre the next moment.

He tried to cry but the tears couldn't come. He was embarrassed as well as anxious. He had wished to speak to them, fight them over this matter and somehow convince them to stop whatever they were planning. Somehow, the words never came out and he felt a strange embarrassment as well as anxiety kick in. ADON-AI... he didn't know what he would do without ADON-AI.

"Listen to me son...we are going to take the fight up to the courts. We are going to win this case. This is our right..." Mrs. Brown spoke to him. He wished he hadn't kept silent by then, watching them helplessly.

"ADON-AI is still a controversial topic all across the world. In Dubai, half the towns are now fully using ADON-AI technology that is allowing rich progress. However, this also means some of the traditional business owners and those who have been earning money by untraditional means are struggling to accept the change. In the other half of the towns and places of Dubai where ADON-AI is not present, people are still clinging to old ways of technology. Most of them have even started a movement based on human centered technology. AFHR might be a terrorist organization, but its agenda is contagious. They have got people to start thinking about the human centered technology. And considering how people have started following ADON-AI as new god in some places, the other movement has only gotten stronger. I believe if you file a report, you will not be just filing a report against three businessmen but rather the entire movement of human centered technologies..." one of the people, whose name was Aslam, explained as he talked to the implant in his own head.

"Remind me again, you have the implant. Why do you even come here?" the other one named Sana asked him as he cleared his throat.

"There is a phenomenon we have come to know as 'neural pathways'. People of different dispositions and personalities or even professions and education levels have different neural pathways which allows them to accept information either more easily or with struggle. You have ADON-AI in your head, but that doesn't mean you will agree to every piece of information that ADON-AI will present to you on a subconscious and conscious level. A health professional will always accept the information based on what they already can relate to based on their knowledge as a medical professional, but they may struggle to understand the technology concepts. In the same way when ADON-AI is giving me therapy at my home, it is not the same. When I come here, my neural pathways are more receptive to the treatment I get from Mrs. Brown and ADON-AI. Both work together. My neural pathways are more accepting of therapy in a more formal setting and so I come for my treatment in this environment. We cannot do everything on our own now can we?" he said with a wink. Being a data scientist, he really gave amazing explanations.

For Ericson though, this was all very hard. He struggled with the concept. They all had a short conversation afterwards and then all went to their homes. He went to his apartment, dreading what was going to happen next. Mrs. Brown gave him a few breathing exercises to keep trying. He was to visualize a few affirmations along with that. Somehow,

ADON-AI was still there, watching his progress and making him feel its presence. But he knew the moment he went home he would feel alone again.

B ack at his apartment, dressed in his evening wear ready for bed, he stared at the empty tv screen and the comfortable bed as he stared at the night lights. Somehow, these lights of this new town always calmed him, but he struggled to understand the concept of therapy. What would happen if the therapy clinic was shut down and he would never get therapy again...breathe easy...breathe...he calmed himself.

A moment later, the doorbell rang, and he was anxious again. Who could that be on his doorstep at this time? He never had any guests. It was 2A.M. He would have to get some sleep and go to work again in the morning.

The doorbell rang again, and he realized there was someone at his doorstep. He had momentarily forgotten it.

"Mr. Ericson if you let us in, we have a grand proposition for you!" the voice came in a familiar tone. He recalled this voice getting into an argument with Mrs. Brown. It was the man with the French beard who had come into that clinic, demanding eviction. Was it a wise choice to let him in?

He was skeptical, grabbing the phone and staging the emergency number in case there came need came for it. There was no reason for him to think that any of them could be there to do harm to him. Why would they? He had left AFHR and the rest of the work was being done by Pakistani ISI in crushing them.

What if they were the last of AFHR members...trying to capture him? Could these three businessmen be related to them? The thought came at the last moment...filling him with crushing anxiety as he opened the door of his apartment. The doorbell rang once more, and the businessmen were about to leave. He carefully held the mobile in his hands, ready to speed dial the emergency number anytime.

"You are Mr. Ericson, right? Sorry for disturbing you at this time but we talked to the main headquarters of the news agency you work in. I got them to get you tomorrow off. I believe we have ample amount of time to discuss the proposition we are going to present to you. What do you say?" the man with French beard named Abdul Hakeem spoke as he stood with two of his associates.

"I...please, come in..." he couldn't stop himself from saying that. To imagine someone coming into your apartment like that when a few moments ago your mind was wanting to fight them...

They came to the main lounge, making themselves comfortable on the couch.

"We will be short now...very short. As you know, we were there at the therapy centre, picking a fight with Mrs. Brown. To be clear, we were just there to discuss the matters with her when she unplugged the socket and came at us with full throttle. Never mind though. I hope we can avoid this lawsuit. It would be inevitable that we would win it, but it would also take some of our valuable time. Now, let me come towards the main point of discussion.

We are introducing a new prototype model of AI. We haven't come up with the name, but it is a new concept. ADON-AI started off as an implant and it ended up killing a lot of people. We all have heard and read the story. It then automatically turned humanitarian? This doesn't make sense now, does it! AFHR was right at first but the moment they started doing those terrorist activities, they became the villains they were so desperately trying to bring down.

Now, the AI model we wish to introduce is a handset. It doesn't get integrated into your head, and it forms a connection with you. Also, it is not alive or a living entity. It is merely...a piece of technology. We humans are meant to rule over technology, not the other way around. That therapy clinic is going down one way or another. If we don't do something, someone else will come and he or she will.

Now onto you...you are the most interesting fellow we have been targeting. ADON-AI refused an implant on you, and we will start our marketing campaign by curing your disorder. We will show the world that our solution is the one that works. It isn't restricted by anything. So, what do you say to coming to our small building tomorrow? Trust me...our AI is focused on medical solutions so it will scan your brain and find the root of the problem. Then, it is onwards towards fixing your mind and personality disorder..." he spoke while pointing towards that building Ericson used to watch every day. He was amazed at that so called "small" building. It towered over his apartment. So that was their place...he imagined their wealth and reach. That was without doubt the tallest building in the entire town of Dubai. He kept staring at it through the giant glass window that provided scenic view of the city. Even at night, the building was lit in blue and red lights all over.

"Alright then...let us go! Mr. Ericson, I believe you will make the right decision!" the businessman beckoned the other two to get up. They once again apologized for meeting at such a late time and then left.

He came back to his room, pondering over the possibility of relying on another AI. Could this be the right decision? He wondered.

He had never considered going to someone else...to someplace else. Ever since he had come here, thanks to a few contacts, he had sought out strong help and it was provided. He had never thought of having another piece of technology tending to his needs. It was not what he had in his mind - ever.

He had a strange fear now lingering over his psyche. He had carried a lavender spray here, but it wasn't going to help...he had a feeling it wouldn't. Sometimes, this feeling came and then it went away.

However, a fear had awakened, and he didn't know what to do now. AFHR...its name shouldn't have been spoken. It had awakened mixed feelings in his psyche. There was the feeling of dread, mixed with the feeling of strange pride...pride that he was gaining the answers. Why feel conflicted when he had been given the answers? Back there...at AHFR, he was given a choice of religions to choose from. The life after death would only be rewarded either with heaven or with hell... Considering how his therapy had been interrupted and how the events were playing out, he wondered if he was giving into the anxiety. The mental defect that was here wasn't going to go away that easily now.

He did the next best thing he could, speaking loudly to the automated system. He knew only when he would return to being himself, he would remember the password.

"Lock down all the systems! Only open with the password!"

ADON-AI wasn't here to help. He knew he would have to calm down, take a few breathing exercises.

"Hello there! May the God of all religions bless you!"

It shook him to the core. Where had this voice come from? That was when he looked at the mirror table...to see his reflection.

Was that his reflection? Or someone in his pajamas, wearing his face and expressions...only with sterner gaze and stricter demeanor. Who was that person?

"Who...who are you?!" he asked, his voice trembling in fear. What was going on?

"Oh...I am you, my dear. Or have you forgotten? Have you really forgotten who you became for a short moment of time?" the reflection asked him.

Sweat poured on his brows, the typical sign of anxiety kicking in. Soon... soon he would be changed, and he wouldn't have any control over it. He hated losing control. Because that meant falling into despair and confusion that he couldn't escape from. And if that happened...

"What are you really afraid of Ericson? I am also you!" the reflection spoke...except that it wasn't the reflection. He felt as if he was the reflection...the actual version of him was someone else...taking over slowly.

He grabbed his own hand, tying it with a handcuff he had hidden beneath his pillow for a time like this.

"You know you cannot tie me up forever...the world needs to be saved. This entire planet needs to be saved. I take pity on you...you have such an important job that you can use to spread enlightenment. You have to use technology to destroy the evil of artificial intelligence. And you falter at the idea of taking over. What happened to the time when you used to preach this philosophy? You spent one and a half months preaching that artificial intelligence was evil! Release me and accept the inevitable!" the voice spoke to him, mimicking his accent and his own tone. Yet he knew very well that this personality wasn't him. It borrowed the worst parts, born out of trauma and suffering and had forged a belief that only thrived by ruthless destruction.

"I was never you willingly! I was forced to take on the character that had nothing to do with me! I will never be you! I will keep you restricted...bound!" he shouted at himself, not knowing what else to do. This version of him was always the worst.

He almost lost his consciousness, seeing his own hand trying to break free of the chain his other hand had bound it with. The other him was slowly taking over now. It was going to break free and try to get out of there...but it wouldn't be able to do so. Only this version of him knew the password to unlock the doors.

The rays of the sun seemed to be reaching him, gently caressing his face. He felt a strange oozy liquid near his nose. The bed that had the handcuff had its support rail broken, viciously attacked as if someone had violently tried to break free. The door of this bedroom had dents on it and the mirror table was in pieces.

This time the episode was violent. He had memories...very vague flashbacks in which he was breaking stuff. The face belonged to someone he vehemently hated. It was his face though...and the figure wearing his face was also him. What had he been seeing?

His nose was dripping. The moment he touched it, he realized that he had a severe nosebleed. No wonder his head felt light, almost dizzying, as if he had a concussion. He wished that he had somehow broken out of this cycle. If he had been given therapy yesterday, this episode wouldn't have happened.

He got up, looking at the unbreakable window glass that had scratches on it. No wonder his other hand had cuts. The heavy chairs in his bedroom had been picked up by his other self and thrown violently at the glass windows.

He had to pack now! There was no going back. He didn't have much time to do anything. He needed to go and get the therapy. But the clinic...the ADON-AI therapy center was closed. Where would he go to?!

He sat down, trying to calm himself. He couldn't. Calming himself now would never help. He knew it now. He had to do something that would actually bring results. For a moment or two, he hated that man named Abdul Hakeem. He was the main reason why his therapy yesterday was disturbed. He hadn't had a violent episode from his other personality taking control for at least eight months. All that progress...crumbled into dust just because he couldn't get one therapy right.

Getting up, he decided he would go to the ADON-AI clinic. He spoke the password that unlocked the doors and deactivated the automated security system. That was something that needed to be done. He had to get that therapy.

Nothing spoke disappointment to him bigger and louder than the closed ADON-AI therapy clinic. He had walked all the way for nothing. The large building that Mr. Abdul Hakeem had showed him stood there right in front of his apartment building, towering over it, mocking his attempt to return to his old source of help. He could see its skyscraper structure, the blue glass that covered the building.

Could that be the solution to his problem? He couldn't tell. All he wanted was to just get it over with. Casting one last disappointed glance at the closed ADON-AI clinic, he realized he had to go to the address that Mr. Abdul Hakeem had told him to go to. He wished for the alternative but there wasn't one. Mrs. Brown was gone, assumably to file a grievance or a lawsuit, hopefully that was the case.

Ericson stood there at the desk, speaking to a European receptionist as she looked critically at this young dark-haired gentleman in grey trousers and checkered white T-shirt. He had now come to know that Mr. Abdul Hakeem wasn't the normal business-man. When he entered through that building, others wondered if he had forgotten the way. When he showed the business card, others looked at him with disbelief and even the reception desk confirmed whether there was someone named Ericson expected that day. Finally, he received the call to go up the elevator.

"Remember dear, be respectful. Sir Abdul Hakeem is known to either make a man's rank higher or break him!" she spoke, chewing that gum and again getting back to the calls she had been receiving.

He wondered where he would be going next. The elevator crossed a lot of floors, nearly thirty-nine of them. When he reached the fortieth floor, he realized that was the floor where he was supposed to meet Mr. Abdul Hakeem.

The elevator opened to a great hall with medical equipment lying around. There were stretchers, chairs with augmented reality helmets on them along with lots of other medical machines he didn't know the purpose for.

He saw Mr. Abdul Hakeem sitting there at the end of the hall. His clothes were in usual white garments while the other two businessmen argued over a point.

The very moment he walked in the door he realized something was amiss. What had they been arguing about?

"I am telling you, that is not what ADON-AI does. Threatening us like that? The call came from an unknown number and the voice resembled the tones that ADON-AI usually speaks in. But...this is not what the AI is known for..." the one with the bald head explained while Mr. Abdul Hakeem listened to him.

"Alright then...Mr. Ericson is here. This proves that we will have the upper hand over our competitor. Mr. Ericson, we have received a special report of your split personality disorder, and we are more than happy to lend a helping hand. Unlike ADON-AI, we will actually have an AI which will actively work with your other side and suppress what doesn't work for your mind... Also, I hope you agree with our methods. This artificial intelligence is like an earpiece which is supposed to cling to your ear and when it does that, your brain is going to be scanned..." Mr. Abdul Hakeem explained.

He was led to one of the chairs with an augmented reality helmet. This was going to be huge, his beating heart told him. He wasn't expecting that kind of high technology to work for him.

There were a few nurses and doctors around him, watching his brain activity on a large screen. Everything started changing the moment he received a special earpiece which he plugged in.

"Greetings, Ericson. I am your personal AI, here to tend your needs. Unlike the ADON-AI implant, you can actually remove me whenever you wish to. I will scan your brain and make this side dominant within you!" the upbeat female electronic voice chimed in his ears.

He closed his eyes, resting on the backseat while feeling its comfort. He knew momentarily that he was safe.

When Ericson woke up, his ear was ringing. He couldn't focus for a moment or two. What was going on? As he looked around, he was still at the same place, but everything was just...changed! He didn't know how, nor could he give any explanation for it.

Mr. Abdul Hakeem and others had disappeared...simply vanished into thin air. A few moments before, they stood there, behind that protective glass while watching his progress in this small cubicle they had prepared by movable boundaries. The doctors that were aiding here were not there anymore. What was going on really?

The lights were all busted, and he realized he was the only one who was there. A frightening aspect! Something was amiss! Where was everyone?

Something sparked, giving him a painful itch in his ears. The ringing started again, and he was frightened. He quickly removed that earpiece, watching smoke rising out of it. Something had happened...his heart could tell. There were a lot of discrepancies that he needed answered.

The iron and zinc that was in that earpiece had been covered with layers of rust. As if it was busted due to something technical. He got up, wanting to go to that elevator and get out of there. This floor had everyone missing and he feared if he stayed there any longer, he would also go missing. It was best to just go to that elevator and find a way down.

His hand ached badly as he reached there, as if he had beaten something with it. There were bruises on his arms. The greatest shock was still awaiting to be discovered. The moment he saw his clothes; he couldn't help but gasp with surprise.

He was wearing what could only be described as a military suit. A military suit?! When had he changed into this outfit? He needed answers. Somehow, the anxiety didn't kick in as he found himself facing a lot of confusion. It was as if there was a sinking feeling in his heart, knowing that something grave had happened. He rushed towards the elevator, pressing its button and activating it.

A spark came out of it. The elevator's door opened, and he stopped himself from stepping into that abyss. The next moment, his heart nearly jumped out of his chest as an elevator dropped, falling with great speed. What was that?! The door of the elevator had opened up, making him see a very deep fall. To think he almost stepped into it...

He calmed himself. Somehow it came easier to him. Somehow...whatever had happened had somewhat cured his anxiety and crippling depression. He wondered how such a thing was even possible...

He took the stairs, not wanting to experience anything else. They were long and he had to admit that manually descending nearly hundreds of stairs just to get from fortieth floor to the first one wasn't the experience he would want to repeat. Dead silence was everywhere...as if the people in this building never even existed.

He wondered if somehow, during the momentary rest he had been given, a great apocalypse came and removed everyone from there. Or perhaps...a great incident occurred, the news of which he was never given the indication of. His mind kept wondering exactly what happened.

Finally, passing through the empty floors, he stepped onto the last one. The receptionist desk was empty. Where was that European lady who had given him the mean stares before sending him to Mr. Abdul Hakeem? Most importantly, where was everyone else? He remembered this gigantic hall-like reception room having a lot of businessmen, chatting while eyeing at him curiously. Where had they all gone? It seemed like months had passed since this place was abandoned. Something was gravely amiss, and he kept wondering about the state of affairs that befell this place. The couches that were placed for the waiting people were all apart. The walls had their paint falling off. That was, however, nothing in comparison to what he saw when he looked at the far end of the reception hall.

The entire building had fallen from that side, looking like the work of a terrible earthquake.

He felt fear...afraid of what was happening around. A feeling lurked inside his chest. Something had passed...and he didn't even know about it. It didn't make sense at all! It never made sense to him in the first place. Ever since the three businessmen walked into that ADON-AI therapy clinic and discussed the deal with Mrs. Brown, threatening her with a lawsuit while planning to shut that place down, something had gone off the rails. He could feel it in his bones.

This was the perfect time to panic...he could tell. He came out of the building to experience the biggest shock of his life. The place...the town of Ar-Raqeem, presented the very definition of a derelict town that had its houses emptied. Where were all the people?

The town had been ravaged, or so that's how everything appeared. He couldn't know what else to say. This place was completely transformed...

The streets which were in perfect alignment with the grey roads were all out of sorts. The wide cracks in the road gave away the appearance of a derelict town. Beautiful shops that he could see everywhere weren't just ravaged...they had been practically crushed. Were there people in there? Oh God! What would have happened if the people were still there when the disaster struck that place?

Something caught his attention. Walking down the broken road across the line of ravaged shops, he found one peculiar place where everything seemed to be fine. Quite an odd occurrence, he told himself. The moment he looked at that shop, his mind weaved different webs of possibilities. This was a simple shop. Different newspapers were there, catching his attention. The moment he picked one up and started reading it, his mind took a direct hit to his sanity.

"16th of October?!" he asked himself the moment he read the newspaper's date. October...how odd that the newspaper was highlighting the month that was six months after...

he vividly remembered the date he had seen on his alarm clock and then his cellphone while coming to this place. It was the 16th of March. Why was the newspaper showing it wrong?

He then saw himself, shaking hands with Mr. Abdul Hakeem. He was the main highlight of the newspaper.

"Mr. Ericson finally leaves his old job behind, taking part in the bigger revolutionary technology to become a reporter for the largest AI firm to directly compete against the ADON-AI system!" he read in the newspaper.

His hands shook and sweat poured on his brows, the typical sign that his sanity was again at stake. What was going on really?! He held his head, shaking it forcefully.

"No! NOOO!" he shouted at the top of his lungs, wanting someone to hear him out. He wanted the police to come to him like they always did if someone was behaving inappropriately in public. To see this hustle and bustle suddenly disappearing and seeing himself alone out here was outright maddening. He needed proof that what he was seeing was just a nightmare, not a reality. He desperately wanted someone or something to come to him and tell him that he was just hallucinating.

He pinched himself on his arms, trying to wake up from this nightmare. He realized the painful truth that there was no nightmare to wake up from in the first place. This was all real!

That was when he found that tape recorder, hidden in a newspaper that was lying on the floor. Wait...wait...a tape recorder?!

It was there all along, hidden in the newspaper, put by someone intentionally. He couldn't help but think as if it was placed there deliberately for him to find it.

Picking it up, he pressed the button to hear his own voice, with stricter tone.

"ADON-AI is the enemy. We are its direct competitors now, so it is pushing our buttons. It is making sure to make our work as hard as possible. It does not matter how humanitarian the AI is believed to be with the actions it is taking right now. We are the first town where the Raqeem AI is being installed. People can do whatever they want to. It is a smart setup which is going to put ADON-AI out of business. The people can actually use it whenever they want to and then unplug it. It follows our commands, and it is making this town progressive. Our everything is advancing at a faster rate. And best of all, it is integrated into an earpiece which is plugged into your ear.

The Raqeem AI has cured my split personality disorder, getting rid of that weaker and unproductive side that always kept me down. I am more alive than ever, and I love doing what I have been doing. The time for new technology is here - it is a new era! I have become everything that I have always wanted to become.

I do feel sympathy for Mrs. Brown who helped me on my initial journey. She was evicted and she lost the case. I felt sorry for her. But then...I realized that ADON-AI wanted to rule over us. It wanted to give us nothing and would force us to take its own perspective. I am really glad I never got an implant. Imagine your own enemy living inside your head. I already had demons and having a demonic entity within, calling itself God, was not going to help me.

I am glad that ADON-AI has been eliminated. But I fear that within that voice that talks to you and puts you in a perfect harmony, there is an evil hidden that only I can see. And of course, Mr. Abdul Hakeem sees it too. We are going to transform this town and we are most definitely going to set an example of how we can have a more progressive, non-invasive AI that rivals ADON-AI - or in some cases, surpasses it. I just hope that ADON-AI doesn't show its true form.

I hope whoever is listening to this, knows that this town is progressing and is prosperous. However, if disaster has struck, then ADON-AI has done what it has been planning to do for a long time!" the recording ended.

The world wasn't stable anymore. He had been feeling intense vertigo since he got out of that building. But finding out something like this...he wondered if he was going to be sane after this. Darkness...over encompassing void...that was what filled his vision. He couldn't take it anymore.

The last thing he saw was the recording playing once more. It seemed he had missed a part of it.

"Then ADON-AI has done what it has been planning to do for a long time. Future me...I am telling you this. ADON-AI is evil. Your trust was misplaced and let me assure you that the ADON-AI is a devil's piece of work. It doesn't take kindly to competitors. If you are hearing this, then it means the worst has already happened...I planned a safety procedure for myself thanks to that earpiece AI...and I hope it worked..."

The lights went out. He couldn't see anything other than a small faint glow of sun, dimming with every moment that was passing. He was going to lose consciousness...

His ears were ringing again. He realized it was already night. Had there not been the automatic lights of streets and billboards, he would have been completely lost into darkness.

The streets were lit and the moment he stood up on his feet, he calmed himself. It was quite odd that the breathing exercises he had been practicing were still working...as if he had been doing them for a long time. He looked around, viewing what could only be described as a broken city night with an illuminated street and the derelict abandoned buildings. Whatever had happened here, thankfully it hadn't taken away the power supply...or whatever was left of it. He could still see a few areas from here, dipped in intense darkness. He wouldn't want to go there, considering the street dogs that roamed there howled with full strength. Who knew what behavior they might have adopted?

He decided to walk now, shaking his head every ten minutes or so. It seemed to help. The inner survivor awakened, and he found himself walking those streets, following the broken trails of streetlights, shops and billboards.

How could it all have happened? This morning was cursed! He knew it! Somehow, there was a mysterious time gap no one could explain. This morning...this very morning! He could remember vividly! Mr. Abdul Hakeem was there, discussing a private matter with his colleagues when he walked in. A matter of a threatening call from ADON-AI...ADON-AI?

Somehow, seeing the darker environment and now remembering that, he was starting to believe that things might not had been what he believed them to be. Perhaps ADON-AI had truly a darker and evil version he hadn't thought about or ever had interacted with. Perhaps that technology was to be blamed... openly! Had this entire town been the victim of ADON-AI's aggression? Did the AI truly cross a line no one thought it would cross?

He was going to pass out once more. Not now, he told himself. He had to get to safety! Possibly find a way out of this town!

Before his senses could fail, he saw something. To say it was a wall would not be enough. It was a gigantic boundary, made up of steel and it separated the other side from this one. What was on the other side? Had the world ended thanks to ADON-AI - the technology that everyone thought was benevolent and kind?

He regretted going near the wall. Before he could touch it, an intense electromagnetic wave sprung forward, making him lose his balance. It spread like a shockwave, effectively darkening the billboards and streetlights around.

It was a frightening aspect...to find yourself suddenly in an unknown place where the hostile environment would be ready to swallow you...

That was what triggered something within him. He realized he had known this place. It had changed that much?

He used to pass from here, every day looking at the blend of cultures depicted through those shops. Those roads...the street started to make more sense than he was realizing. This place...it had an ADON-AI clinic at the end!

He looked at the far end of this place, looking briefly at the only billboard that was illuminated. The rest of the street was engulfed into darkness. He couldn't tell if it was fate or just an intriguing coincidence. He read the billboard properly.

"ADON-AI Therapy Centre" the billboard said. That was the only closed shop that stood there. Behind him, the steel wall that extended across the entire town made another noise, putting him into an alert mental state. He feared that the shockwave might return, and this time it might be fiercer. He was standing again too close to the wall once more...

He ran forward towards that only illuminated billboard. He managed to get away from that steel wall that stood there, separating this side from the other one. He wondered what lay there on the other side... the dark suspense combined with anxiety outright nullified his senses.

The billboard was still like that...the way it was yesterday...or if the time gap was considered...the way it was on March 15th. Oddly enough, it was the only thing that stood there, unchanged with the flow of time. The billboard had gotten a little rusty, but the color and the brightness was still the same.

It invoked strange insecurity and fear in him. He realized he had once come here...a mild flashback occurred...something that made him highly uncomfortable. His heart beat faster than usual. He saw someone pressing strange buttons...who was that man in the black and white suit? Mrs. Brown was tied up, sitting right in front of him as that faceless man disabled the implant in her...killing her in the process.

He couldn't take it anymore. What he could do was to run away and never look back. He needed to find his apartment. There wasn't much thinking involved after he saw that vision in bits and pieces. Something had happened inside the ADON-AI therapy clinic that he couldn't remember. That faceless man was the real culprit. He had only one name dripping off his lips.

"ADON-AI!" he whispered to himself. That faceless man had somehow a link to ADON-AI, he could tell. And somehow...his mind started feeling an intense grief...an almost traumatic response.

The moment he saw the ramshackle building of his apartment was when he finally gave up. He wanted a shelter, and he had found one. Hopefully, his room would still be there. If he could only get a good night sleep, maybe this all would be over. What if this was all a side effect of that ear-piece AI he had plugged in? What if this entire place was just a nightmare and getting to his bed would be the end of it all? His mind spun so many ideas that now he questioned reality. The moment he stumbled and mildly skinned his knees, he realized it was a very convincing nightmare. More reason for him to keep on going towards the room where he slept. Perhaps he would find answers there that he so desperately sought.

He finally reached in front of the building that miraculously still stood there. There, at the second story, he had his apartment. The topmost floors had fallen in.

He struggled with the idea of going on. This was too much for him...it clouded his judgment of safety. He needed to find his room...one way or another!

There was a rubble gathered there. Thoughts of what might have happened flooded his mind. He was unable to process for a moment or two. The amnesia returned again, and he struggled to remember. He was here this morning...seeing everything from a different perspective. When had the building taken such a hit? What transpired here that missed his attention? He never knew. No matter how much he wished to remember, the memory was absent.

He entered that building, resisting a lot of things that were on his mind. ADON-AI...could it really have turned evil? He dared not go to the elevator even though it was miraculously functional still. What if something happened in the middle of his ascent? There would be no one to help him.

He rushed towards the stairs. He had to move there and see for himself. The flickering lights and dark ambience made him nervous but that wasn't his concern. He hurried across those stairs that used to belong to a well-structured apartment.

He struggled to ascend through the stairs. They had been made up of concrete and apart from a few cracks, they were mostly alright. However, his head throbbed with an intense headache, as if he had ascended and descended these steps at least a thousand times. And that was within this time span that was somehow absent from his memory. He kept ascending till he reached to the second floor.

There was a brief episode of violent flashes, all passing through his mind uncontrollably. He had been coming here and that was in the time span he had no memory of. After March 16th, something had changed and that something was also responsible for his current memory loss. If only he could remember!

The apartments were quite old fashioned. He still felt very creepy standing there all alone, watching the first four stories of this place illuminated. Some apartments had power blackouts, but the rest were all lit...as if all the lights had been turned on. He couldn't have it any other way as the alternative would be him, standing in an intense blackout situation and that wouldn't be very encouraging.

At the end of the floor, he could see something...like a figure. Even though he was all alone, it was frightening. He moved slowly, hoping that he wasn't alone. That figure was there, lying on the floor with a bed sheet on it, right in front of the opened door of an apartment. He kept on walking, forgetting that he had passed in front of his own apartment.

The moment he reached there was when he regretted coming closer. Even though a bedsheet was spread out there and covered that figure lying on floor, he could feel the bones...there was no flesh. Just bones. This was a skeleton!

He gasped with fear, turning back and seeing his own apartment. It didn't take him long to reach to his own place and lock the door from the inside. Whatever was going on here, he couldn't take it anymore.

He lit up his apartment and turned on all the lights. He needed all those lights on! The darker alternative would be to stand in a complete blackout. Given the circumstances, he would soon have a heart attack if he stood in immense overwhelming darkness.

He saw his own living room, where he had hosted Mr. Abdul Hakeem for a brief moment. There at the dining table, he found a journal. Picking it up, he soon found himself struggling. Who was the one who had filled these pages? He couldn't remember.

The handwriting was in italics, and he struggled to remember if he ever had developed the ability to even write like that. He didn't even have a journal.

The first page caught his attention as he saw a strange diagram. Was it a machine? Some sort of device that whoever owned this journal had designed?

He didn't know the answers, nor could he give an explanation to what this journal was doing in his living room. All he knew was that there was this diagram of a generator-like device with its name written in Italic.

"Electromagnetic pulse generator..." it read. Where had that journal come from in the first place? He found himself skimming through the italic handwriting. At the end, he found a bold statement,

"Today is the day I do it! Today is when it all shall be how it is supposed to be!"

He again struggled to remember and to his disappointment, he found his mind blank. It seemed almost like it was yesterday since he was sitting here, listening to the businessman with his French beard and his two colleagues who looked more like his assistants, agreeing to whatever he was saying.

His room! There might be clues there! He quickly got up, moving to his room while looking around. The lights were on there too and to his surprise, there was no bed nor the mirror table. There was a big mirror though, right in front of him.

A strange episode of amnesia struck him as he struggled to look at his own reflection. The almond eyes stared back at him, with similar raven hair and a fair-skinned face. And was that a clean shave? He remembered he always had stubble.

He always saw the other personality, dying to come out. This time, there was nothing. The other side felt like it never existed. He had to admit. Amidst the madness that went on, this was the first thing that he could perceive as normal. The rest of the bedroom was filled with briefcases. He opened them one by one.

A strong scent of gunpowder filled the air. He couldn't tell if this was his room or if it belonged to someone else. Where had this gunpowder come from? Its smell was terrible, and he couldn't tell when was the last time he had smelled this much gunpowder. It was when he was...

He tried not to remember but the memories again bombarded him with intensity. He used to be someone else when he was with AFHR. He couldn't help but remember that they had given him special training. And his other brainwashed version had learned that training in a short time. What had they taught him? He remembered his habit of journaling. The handwriting he used to have was something similar to an italic font...

Sweat poured on his brows, and he started shaking. This was too much! Still too much for him! Was he the one who had written that journal? How had he designed a perfect diagram of an electromagnetic pulse generator?

That was when he saw something. Right there at the corner, he could see what was going to provide some answers for him. A black laptop was there - plugged into the socket. He wondered how it had been present there all this time. As he looked at it, he saw the dark screen and opened tabs. Whoever had been using this laptop had been using the dark web and gathering information and creating lists. He could see a few contacts listed as AFHR officials.

The moment he logged in as the password had been saved, he received a few unopened messages,

"Listen to me now! This can take your life but rest assured, you will emerge victorious. Maybe you are the messiah we all had been waiting for!"

"Today is the day God embraces you as his child as you will bring down ADON-AI and the earpiece AI also known as Raqeem technology. The fate of this Ar-Raqeem town will surely be a lesson for ADON-AI and other AI' s that plan to subjugate humanity"

"You are doing God's work! Keep doing it..."

He got back, looking at himself in the mirror once more. Had he been doing it all? Was he the one who had initiated the plan to execute?

There on the screen of that black laptop, he saw another tab opened. He clicked on it and to his horror, he saw the schematics of the electromagnetic pulse generator. There was an entire parts list that had been gathered, all of them collected using a masterplan and a procedure. In the end, the final step was to mount it on the signal tower of the Raqeem building, the place of Mr. Abdul Hakeem.

He got up, wanting to get answers. Tears were falling out of his eyes, and he wanted to stop this amnesia. He got out of there, rushing his steps to the stairs and from there, he got on his way towards the main road. The sky was pulsating with a dark azure texture. Dawn was approaching. He didn't know how much time had passed.

He finally ran on the road, stopping in front of the building where he had come this morning. He wasn't going to count the time now! For him, he had walked just this morning into that building.

There wasn't much to be seen. He rushed towards the reception table and discovered that the signaling room was on the side that had collapsed. Yet there was a vision once more which led him to kneel and let out another gasp of pain. The faceless man he had been seeing in his visions had come here along with the rest of the people. Who were they?

Armed and holding dangerous guns? They held the entire Ar-Raqeem town hostage, or so his visions unveiled to him. There were mass murders...

He couldn't deny it anymore. All he wanted were a few answers and it seemed they were all eluding him. There was a last thing that he remembered, and it overwhelmed him and shook him to the core. That faceless man he had been seeing also went to the ADON-AI clinic...it went blur from there but there was something he managed to remember. In the ADON-AI clinic, something was still operational. He knew there was something there that held answers to his questions. Something...or someone was buried there.

He got up now, shaking his head to keep those visions away. Hopefully, they wouldn't bother him much now. But on the inside, he was no longer completely ignorant, and he was utterly devastated. A dark confession had been conjured up and he knew that when it would come out, come to light, that he would then be completely shattered.

He was standing right in front of the ADON-AI clinic. From there, all he needed to do now was to confront whatever demon was hiding there. It didn't take too much force to try and break down the front door. It fell apart, giving in to the heavy stones he threw along with rust that had collected with time.

The first thing he saw was a skeleton with female clothing. On back of her skull, there was an implant. A thought emerged through his mind as he took a socket nearby and plugged it in that implant. He had remembered that Mrs. Brown used to do that. He tried not to think who the skeleton belonged to. That would throw him off balance.

The entire place shook for a moment or two. He tried to reverse the procedure, but it was in vain. Whatever he had set in motion had now been permanent. Even when he removed the socket, the system of this entire clinic was running.

A monitor screen scrolled down and from there, he heard a friendly voice,

"Ericson...is that really you?" ADON-AI spoke.

He collapsed. To see it all…to face it alone, knowing the news that ADON-AI had done something evil…to force yourself to stay sane during the influx of emotions that went on through his head…it was all in his mind…

When he heard that friendly voice…he simply collapsed. Like a child who had heard the voice of a supportive friend for the first time in so long, he knelt on ground, crying in a loud voice.

"ADON…please help me…I woke up here…ADON, I don't think you did this! ADON, please! ADON…ADON…" he spoke, breaking into tears. Screw whatever he had heard…

"My dear, you are in trauma. I am guessing Thomas is gone now… Listen, I have opened that room for you. I cannot control the environment or what exactly you'll see as you make your way there… but just go there…there are explanations for all this, and I believe you are ready!"

He got up. Whatever was going to happen, it couldn't be worse than what he had been thinking. A part of him trusted ADON-AI, even if it had gone evil. He had no desire to do anything other than what that AI told him. He had somehow formed an emotional connection to ADON-AI. He wasn't ready to do anything other than follow its directions. He headed towards the room, the door of which had recently opened for him. He ignored all of the closed rooms in his way. The mind had lost the ability to think and analyze now. He knew he had heard that recording about ADON-AI being the devil technology. However, his mind lost the ability to think critically and the moment he heard a friendly voice, everything that was questioning ADON-AI within him collapsed.

He went to that room, bracing himself for whatever was coming next.

"I have chosen a series of recordings that will help you process whatever has happened. I believe if I tell you directly, you will enter a dangerous level of shock which might be even fatal for you. Within these six months, big changes had come…" ADON-AI grew silent afterwards as another screen emerged from the top, extending in front of him.

He saw himself, getting up after the earpiece had been given to him. When had that happened? He remembered that morning vividly. That was all he could remember. He had gone to the building of Mr. Abdul Hakeem where he had met him for a procedural brain scan. That was all he could remember. Then who was this young man, wearing his face and walking towards his apartment?

"The earpiece AI was a symbiotic AI that was trying to help you with your personality disorder. There was a reason why I never agreed to give you an implant, Ericson. Your other side of the personality was too dominant in one case. It emerged too forcefully, not giving you time to develop resistance against it. Therefore, when your brain was scanned and the earpiece AI was given to you, it accidentally switched personalities, and your other side was activated. This was the event that cascaded a series of future events, all of them leading to hundreds of deaths and, ultimately, the overall destruction of this town!

Your other side was very strong and unfortunately, the earpiece technology only gave a more dominant hand to the more destructive you. Instead of bringing this human side of you to surface, the earpiece technology only suppressed this weaker side which is currently you. That version of you started calling himself Thomas secretly..." ADON-AI stopped for a moment to give Ericson time to process and adjust.

His mind was numb...like a person whose entire world was falling apart, and he could just observe it. Not able to do anything other than... just... observe it and wonder what he ever did to deserve this. He always questioned the presence of God. But could he now put this blame on Him?

Another event started playing on the monitor. Ericson remembered that there was a camera in his apartment. ADON-AI had accessed it somehow.

He saw himself, writing plans on that journal. His face told a story of someone who was planning something big. That version of him sat down, pondering deeply. Then, that version of him got up, turning on a new black laptop. He started speaking,

"I have recently got a new job offer from Mr. Abdul Hakeem. God gave me this opportunity to now come to the surface and finally suppress the weaker version of me. I have started calling myself Thomas. I have heard that AFHR members are present on the dark web. I will contact my brothers and see what can be done. I want to punish the AI and every piece of technology that is present here! This AI needs to be stopped!"

The video ended as ADON-AI again gave him a brief pause to collect his thoughts. Ericson kept descending into darkness, not knowing what he would do other than stare blankly at the screen and think about ending his own life. Could he do that? He could grimly see where this was going.

"Your other version contacted AFHR. That is when it all started. They were going to make this town an example of what they could do. It was supposed to send a message. Therefore, through the dark web, Thomas started taking lessons from the AFHR members, asking them about his plan. That was when Mr. Abdul Hakeem offered Thomas a job opportunity in his firm. That was also when Thomas started raising his voice against me, trying to shut down this clinic that still kept running. He knew he couldn't. Therefore, he, and the AFHR members that were in contact with him, started planning something big..." ADON-AI stopped explaining, noticing the clear change that was within his expressions.

He felt a dark calmness prevailing his senses. He knew where this was going...he was still processing what he would do next, but he just didn't wish to make a final decision without giving up. His mind was exhausted already. However, he knew at the final moments of this session... the moment it ended... he only had one thing he wanted to do. There was only one thing on his mind. Now... how to execute that one thing? He didn't know.

Another video played which made him realize that two months after he had gotten the earpiece, the town was still thriving. It had easily become one of the largest hubs for trading and cultural exchanges. The town had only become securer and better.

In the video, he saw the other version of himself, standing right beside Mr. Abdul Hakeem while giving a loud speech. In front of him, there were a lot of cameramen who were standing and jockeying for position to get the best shots.

"I know these are big changes, but I had an illness that ADON-AI couldn't solve. This Raqeem AI had been there on my side. It helped me cure my split personality disorder and I feel finer than ever before. The best part about it? We know ADON-AI is always an imposed solution. It never logs off, never gets removed, for if it does get removed, it will kill you.

Now here, this earpiece technology is so amazing that whenever you wish to remove it, you can easily do so. Without any complexities..." he spoke while trying to take off the earpiece. There was a certain problem as he tried his best but couldn't do it. To keep the impression consistent, Mr. Abdul Hakeem took off his earpiece, showing everyone how it was done.

"That was the first hint for Thomas, the destructive version of you. You will realize later what happened. Thanks to the information Thomas provided to the dark web contacts, AFHR sent their agents here, disguised as great businessmen. Mr. Abdul Hakeem was very oblivious to everything. He was just under the impression that ADON-AI had been rivaled with a superb technology that he had invented. For him, his campaign of removing me from this town and instead introducing his earpiece AI was everything.

That was when concerns started to rise. Earpiece AI had somewhat destructive effects in some cases. In patients with dementia, there was a report from one among the hundred patients that instead of curing the dementia, the earpiece technology had started giving them another personality. The patients didn't actually get cured of their dementia. The brain part that was responsible for dementia formed another personality that started to rise at least once a month. When one of those patients took his life, this concern finally came to the surface.

That was when Mr. Abdul Hakeem started to develop a greedier and somewhat obsessive attitude with his progress. Earpiece AI had potentially provided the cure for brain tumors and some other brain diseases. However, that was everything that I could do as well in a jiffy. His aim was to do everything he could to highlight the things that ADON-AI couldn't do, and that the earpiece technology could. Therefore, this also meant making Thomas his main icon and spokesperson.

He was unaware of a far sinister plot that was at play. Blinded by his greed, he finally listened to the suggestion from Thomas and the other businessmen that were AFHR members in disguise that boundaries needed to be erected, and ADON-AI's influence would have to be eliminated within these walls.

Luckily, I was able to connect myself to the apartment where you lived, and I was able to log in to the dark web. I alerted the military and intelligence services, providing them solid proof that the disguised businessmen were actually terrorists. Of course, there was a limitation. I had to personally ask Mrs. Brown to plug into the socket of the mainframe to access the internet. My access had been limited thanks to their malwares. Mrs. Brown won a case in which she still owned the ADON-AI clinic. But the rest of the people with implants had been evicted off their properties. This made Mrs. Brown a bigger target. I, however, had integrated myself into the town's mainframe and I became a part of it too.

Unfortunately, Thomas and his fellows had already constructed their electromagnetic pulse generator - what they thought could effectively bring down the entire AI system and kill everyone with the earpiece AI. They would then use it on my implants too. However, I had logged into his dark web account and found out the frequency they were using. Unfortunately, I was too late. When I found out about this, Mrs. Brown had been killed, and the generator had been activated. The electromagnetic pulse generator worked too well, killing some of the people in the town and destroying buildings with its shockwaves. The rest were killed by Thomas who led AFHR agents into the building, brutally killing the other survivors off. All of this was done to show the world that a terrorist organization still remained which would bring death upon those who accepted AI into their lives. Of course, their victory was short lived. I raised the frequency of my implants and led an army of agents into this town. The pulses of that generator wouldn't harm my implants then. Thomas hid himself and was presumed dead but the rest of AFHR agents were killed. However, when this all ended, this town was forever abandoned, the survivors moving to other places of Dubai. This is a ghost town now" ADON-AI stopped.

"My god... I remember now... I was in his subconscious, watching it slowly. Thomas realized the dark truth behind his earpiece technology. That was the irony. He was only on the surface because the earpiece AI made him do so. I was the conscious and he was the subconscious even though he wasn't meant to be. He was overly dependent on his earpiece technology. When the electromagnetic pulse generator worked, he realized he had only a few more days left to live. The earpiece AI was the only thing that allowed him to come up to surface. When it was destroyed, I finally surfaced up. So he then goes and sets a recording for me to listen to, trying to make me think you were the villain. And then... he finally returned to that medical room where he had originally come into power... he wanted to expire there... oh..." Ericson groaned and got up. He had finally made up his mind.

"Where are you going, Ericson? Listen to me...I know what you are thinking. I can help you. Thomas is gone now, and he is never coming back. Your split personality is never going to return. You don't have any part in this!" ADON-AI spoke.

He wasn't listening. He just wanted to find something sharp. He found a piece of glass. His eyes teared up at the notion, but he wasn't going to stop now. This needed to be done.

"You have been a friend ADON. I don't know if I would have survived without you. However, I cannot forgive my other self's transgressions...I believe I must pay for them!"

As he spoke, he slowly brought that piece near his throat. It was sharp, making his hands bleed. But he tightened his grip's strength, wanting to follow through with what he believed he had to do.

"You are ready for an implant. Trust me and I will help you. Thomas is not your fault, Ericson!" ADON-AI tried to convince him to change his mind.

He thought about it for a moment or two. What was he going to do then? He then smiled at ADON-AI, bringing that sharp piece of glass to his throat.

"Goodbye, my friend. I hope humanity realizes how important you truly are!" he spoke and then embedded that sharp glass into his throat.

There was a flickering of lights, a clear indication that ADON-AI was grieving. Yet it couldn't stop the flow of blood that soon made Ericson close his eyes forever.

Act V: The Gospel of Gabriel

GREAT BRITAIN

A nyone could have recognized that building with the "Clarity Order Department" name on the front of it. That triangular building was known for its seemingly random experimentations as well as new breakthroughs. However, no one had expected what would happen on that fateful day. A strong, focused indigo beam shot into the sky, causing the purple lightening to emerge. It seemed to have come out of every single sci-fi apocalyptic motion picture everyone has seen before. This unnatural event struck fear into the hearts of citizens, as they saw formations of strong hurricanes in the vicinity of that beam.

There, staring at the questioning ant-like figures of those citizens, he stood on the top floor. His mind constantly raced with ideas on what to do next. Idiots! All of them were idiots! They were like sheep who had found a perfect shepherd. These people allowed ADON AI, a devilish technology, to be their new ruler. Three entire continents! The more he thought about it, the more his heart sunk into the deep grief. The apocalypse everyone talked about and fantasized about in those sci-fi movies had truly come - and none of these people knew it.

His name was William Bowstalk, the head scientist as well as entrepreneur in charge of the Clarity Order Department, a place known for its inventions. He felt like the puppet in this big world controlled by something much bigger than him. And he never liked it! To think that ADON-AI had implemented laws that prevented anyone from engaging in experiments related to artificial intelligence! That devilish technology had taken over everything! Strict laws had been implemented across the three continents that were newly formed under the banner of ADON-AI. It ruled over them with an iron hand and effectively removed all those that questioned its rule. Not him though! He would keep questioning the devil's rule even if it meant his own end! The worst part was...ADON-AI had invoked either respect or fear. There never was struggle or resistance. He knew what this technology had done. It had killed all possibilities of rebellion. He had truly thought it was quite a clever dictatorship. It had taught either fear, or respect, but never rebellion.

Nonetheless, the spark of rebellion could never die down. It lived on in his inventions even though he was given room for as limited exposure as possible. Through those human centered inventions, he had made it clear that a human controlled internet was all they needed. He still remembered passing along very strong-worded comments about ADON-AI in that TV program that hosted him. The public still wondered about why he hadn't experienced the repercussions. If he were a common man, he would have been sent to the rehabilitation camp where his mind would be conditioned. Remembering some details about that particular TV appearance, he let himself gaze upon that city.

He looked down upon this sheep of a city that had somehow started using the ADON-AI induced network, exploring the facilities his human-centered internet wasn't able to provide. The room where he watched that purple lightning was at the top, providing him the perfect view of the sky that looked like it was hosting some kind of catalytic reaction. He smiled at the aspect of it. The unstable lightning that fell on the ground nearby, destroying some of the cars was a perfect indication representing his hatred for the city that chose ADON-AI's technology over his.

The moment the beam charged up that machine he had built, he simply exited the room, taking off his coat and his shirt. He was ready for what came next, ready for his body to be disintegrated into a digital consciousness program. The idea had never been tested properly, and he had lost two of his promising assistants before, but it was all worth it! Adjusting his hearing aid, he made his mind ready for the future plans. There were a lot of them!

He exited the room, thinking about the right decision of giving the staff a leave of absence today. To his closest circle of employees, he had handed several tickets for outer city travel. What was going to come wasn't something that they would be ready to witness. He finally came across that spiral staircase, leading towards a hall. He ascended the long staircase, finally reaching that hall that was built further up on top of the building. There, the scientists used to harness the natural lightning for their experiments. He still kept his intense stare at the rotating pillar-like machine as it projected the purplish beam onto the sky.

William threw an intense stare at this machine. After a while, this machine was going to achieve everything he had ever hoped for or dreamed for. Something big was about to happen and this city would soon be convinced in his ideals. Sometimes, a big revolution could only come with something drastic and earthshaking, he used to tell himself. This was the earthshaking machine that would soon make people question everything!

That was when his cellphone rang. The caller made his lips widen into a sarcastic smile. He accepted the call, placing the phone just rightly on his ears.

"You will not get away with this!" the voice was of someone he didn't wish to meet in person. He responded while smiling.

"Oh, but I already have! That purple lightning you see? It is just an indication of the greatness I am going to achieve. None of you will be here to stop me! And don't bother sending any implant soldiers under the banner of that devil ADON-AI! I have set up electromagnetic traps. If any of you enter, the traps will go off and anyone with the implant will die!" he chewed on every word, making his intentions clear.

"I am still giving you a chance William! Surrender. We are not bad people. We are merely those who don't want to see any more children, women or men dying...more wars happening!" the voice was quite convincing, yet his sarcastic smile deepened.

"I recognize your voice. They hosted once a television program on how you were beyond redemption. How your psychology was hell bent on killing women and children. You called yourself the killer Billy. I know that you committed at least sixteen murders. The death penalty was on the table. Choosing the death penalty or choosing an implant of ADON-AI. You should have hung! But now... you live...with that abomination in the back of your head..." William spoke, throwing a curious stare at the city below.

"Ok then...now let me drop the garb of this man I am possessing. I believe in the death penalty too. But I also believe in a penalty where I can make a person change. Through this implant, I am controlling his mind as he is serving in one of my units. However, at the same time, I am redesigning his psychology. He is reliving the experiences of the murders. He is feeling the pain of his victims on an everyday basis. But at the same time, he is serving humans in a better way. Worse than death? Possibly, but overall, a better fate for the whole of mankind than putting him underground. For you though, you have devised worse ways for yourself. A dark fate will await you...if you don't stop what you are doing, punishment awaits you!" the one on call suddenly dropped all niceties, taking on a more sinister tone. His voice was cold and calculating.

"Ah...my old nemesis! I have always hated you ADON-AI. You take over the minds of others. You bend others to your will. You are a tyrant now...someone who cannot take critique or harsh opinion. After this one experiment, I will change everything. This new perfect human vessel doesn't have any of your implants. He is a perfect specimen for my kind of experiment. And don't you dare talk about moralizing!" he spoke one final time before dropping that cell phone and stomping on it. No more delays!

"This is going to end badly..." the cell phone spoke. It spoke in a monotonous tone, almost sounding like a machine...a computerized female voice could be heard as the phone uttered a few words.

"*I AM HERE!*"

William looked at it with hate. He kicked that phone harder as it struck the wall, breaking into a few pieces. However, he knew it wouldn't do good now. His hand moved willingly, and he beat up his own head for that folly. How could he do something so stupid?!

"By making that call, I didn't know you were sending a signal here! You bastard! You accessed the frequency of my channel and transported yourself by matching data frequencies with the electronics... in my building! Argh! Now you are inside here!" William spoke with hatred filling up his voice. He always hated the ADON-AI and right now, he wanted nothing but to make this building explode with ADON-AI in it.

"You don't understand that my reach is everywhere. I keep on evolving with new ways to transform my data every day. Now, I shall personally deactivate this machine and stop whatever madness you are planning, William!" the ADON-AI's voice rung into his head. He felt as if he had an implant. He then realized that his hearing aid was being used.

"I will never let you win ADON-AI!" the voice became quite scornful as he quickly went forward to deactivate the machine. That was when his hearing aid responded with an intense sound, as if a screech was aimed directly into his ears.

"You...are...up...to...your....old tricks again!" William spoke while trying to detach the hearing aid. His head was ringing for a few moments. Holding it together, he struggled to move towards that machine, the wires around that device coming all alive. They wrapped around his legs, creating a moment of struggle for him. He was frozen into one place as he forced his legs to move forward despite the wires restricting his movements.

"I cannot let you deactivate my machine. It is the only thing that will end your tyranny. You mind control people, and you have caused tremendous amounts of death. Do you have any idea of what will happen if this machine is deactivated?" William spoke, chewing on every word. He tried to remove his hearing aid, but his arms were now covered with restricting wires too.

"This machine is the root of evil and nothing can be more severe than its success. As for mind control, just wait and see what I have in store for you. In my world, humans don't die early. They die of natural causes of old age and that is all. As for me being a tyrant, what is wrong with exercising my will on people? They are not my slaves...they are my children, and every child needs a parent!" ADON-AI's voice was polite as it reverberated through his hearing aid. He knew that the machine would be destroyed. Its internal mechanisms were fried and now, the purple lightening was disappearing. The systems were shutting down.

"You don't understand ADON. The machine is important. Half of the technology of Bloomsburry city is linked to this building. Consequences of destroying something this vital could be disastrous. You said you protect humanity. Think about the repercussions of what you are doing!" William tried to make a convincing point. He knew ADON-AI had one weak point and that was preserving humanity. It might have taken the form of a dictator that ruled over the people with an iron hand, but nonetheless, it still protected humans whenever possible.

However, none of these thoughts were proved right as William heard a very sinister tone of voice that ADON-AI adopted.

"I know what is going on William. And I don't allow it. If this machine succeeds, many people have the probability of dying. The consequences are not that dire if I deactivate this machine!" ADON-AI spoke.

Away from the triangular figure of that building, strange flashes seemed to appear in the sky. The unnatural thunder moved like it had a mind of its own, manifesting itself into a lightning bolt that felt on the ground nearby. It was a heartrending sight as the entire sky seemed to have come alive, showering the lightning bolts everywhere within the vicinity of that building. Panic spread like wildfire as people came out of their houses, taking to the road and running or driving away from the sight of that horror.

The citizens of Bloomsburry felt tremors in the land near the triangle Clarity Department building. Something sinister was going on there!

No one expected the disaster that came in the next moment. The earth near that place shattered, swallowing the entire line of houses and cars parked nearby. It didn't stop there, the road erupting with fountains of lava beneath...the area near that building had soon turned into a sight from hell...casualties were heavy!

The alarm was ringing with a loud and annoying noise. He wanted to slam his fist down on top of it and break it. But then, he would have to go to market and buy a new alarm clock...just like the last four times. The doctor had specifically asked him to control his temper. Ever since that incident...

He tried not to think about it. His heart was heavy with grief, and he couldn't remember the last time he had smiled. He got up, thinking about plenty of reasons to go back to sleep. He got up nonetheless, staring at the mirror table at some distance. Finally, with a jerk, he pulled himself off the bed, letting his sleek figure land his feet on the sandals. He put them on and rubbed his eyes, moving towards that mirror table. He needed to comb his hair and get ready for that big day. He moved in front of that mirror, welcoming a tired man with circles beneath his black eyes. He hadn't slept properly for days. The stubble on his round face was thick and the brown hair was all messed up. Another wretched day...to go and work in that industry...

That was when he realized. Today was Sunday. He had the day off... This means he could walk around the town and explore. It would be good for his mental health...just like the doctor had suggested. The doctor had also suggested to remind himself to think of a reason to smile. And if he couldn't, he would simply have to smile without reason. Still...he couldn't. Those were golden words...simply fantasy words with no real practicality at all. If the doctor knew about his life...how much he had lost ever since that fateful day...

Grief ate his heart. He looked into that mirror and saw his tears rolling on his cheeks. His poor wife and daughter ...both were in that house that day, waiting for him to return. Then, hell broke loose the moment lightning struck the ground. He never would have known that finding and buying their dream home near the landmark building of the Clarity Department would be a death sentence for him and his family. How *could* he ever have even known that?

He couldn't! Tears kept rolling down his cheeks as he found himself unable to process the grief. It came and went...just like it always did. Putting on the casual white T-shirt and loose grey trousers, he remembered how much therapy had helped him during these three years of loss. At first, he couldn't think properly, crying uncontrollably anywhere. He knew he never had any choice in that matter. However, thanks to the aid given by ADON-AI, he soon received an implant and started gaining more mental help. Still, it wasn't enough. The implant was great. It kept his mental hormones in balance and often soothed his aching head. And it allowed him to cry regularly, washing away his grief. Not that he needed to cry everyday now.

He threw one last stare at the two-room apartment attached with a bathroom and then came out, locking the door. Avoiding the elevator like he always did, he used stairs. Last time when it all happened, he was in the elevator, watching the city falling apart through the glass walls. The elevators had become his phobia ever since. He took stairs always, watching that glass elevator with fear. The moment he came out of that apartment building, he stared at the busy street. Then, he stared straight to the left.

It was always a dilemma, and somewhat a worrying factor, for him to notice the fallen debris of forty houses near his apartment. Somehow, he still hadn't moved away from the place where the Clarity Department's triangular building stood. Or whatever was left of it. Perhaps he still had hope somewhere in his damaged psyche that around that triangular building that was surrounded by a gigantic circular impact crater, his wife and daughter would still crawl out. The circular crater that covered the ruins of the Clarity Department was huge with a soil that had turned black. In those frozen lava rocks, the remains of what once formed debris of fallen houses could be seen. Why hadn't anything been done about it? He walked away from the busy street, heading in the opposite direction. His steps stopped at the edge of the impact crater, looking down below. That was when he heard steps. Someone was approaching him from behind. As he turned his head, his mouth whispered the words, "Old Billy".

Old Billy was a sixty-year-old man, twice his age. He had a bulky physique and a bald head with a trimmed beard. He knew old Billy had something to say. This man had an implant and always gave the best advice in his warm and affable tone. He almost looked like Santa, his red sweater covering the grey shirt, tucked inside his black trousers.

"How are you, Gabriel?" Old Billy asked, his grey eyes inspecting the slouching figure of a thirty-year-old Gabriel who gave an empty stare to that building.

"I am alive...isn't it ironic that the Clarity Department destruction is visible to the left side whereas if we look to the right, we see something like a busy street. Makes me wonder about the cycle of life and death..." Gabriel waxed on in a bit of a daze as he looked at the fallen building.

"I assure you about one thing. It wasn't your fault that... you know what I mean. Listen, if you need some time, you can stay here and watch it for a while. I know it calms you down...gives you closure... some sort of. And when you are done, I will be in that restaurant, ordering your favorite pastrami sandwich meal deal...also, step a little away. You are standing really close to the edge of that crater!" Old Billy spoke before patting him warmly and moving in the opposite direction to the street. He was quite shaken too every time he saw that ruin. Gabriel wondered why Old Billy was so kind to him. The implant in the back of his head was visible as Old Billy walked in the opposite direction. Was it because of the implant that this sixty-year-old man was his new companion? Did ADON-AI turn him into a kind and compassionate person? He knew that Old Billy used to be a fugitive from justice once. Until he got that implant. Then, he became one of the best law-abiding citizens. For a moment or two, Gabriel's sight faded, and he soon found himself struggling with a strange vertigo. It was as if he could see it all...the visions of death and destruction as many houses were destroyed in that event.

That was when he heard strange whispers...as if something was calling him there. Something very strange was happening. He tried to look around, trying to find that person who was whispering to him. It was to no avail. He was dangerously close to that impact crater's edge. That was when he realized his vision was getting blurred and his steps were not under control. He wished he hadn't come so close to the edge of the crater as he slipped and fell straight into the crater. Luckily, the slip wasn't fatal, and the fall was broken quickly due to sand that had gathered there. He landed safely though his mental state was shaken for a while.

"What the hell..." he spoke as he soon found himself a few meters down from where he was standing. He was lucky...very lucky to be standing on this edge. If he had been standing somewhere different, he would have been seriously injured.

Fear...it was what filled his mind as he got up quickly, thanking whoever was responsible for his unexpected luck. He looked for a way out. At some distance, there was a slope that led upwards to the busy street. He promised himself that next time, he would sightsee from there. Before he could move there, something like a strange whisper caught his attention. The moment he looked around, he saw something like a tablet, lying around.

"Pick me up!"

He could have ignored that device if it hadn't whispered to him. The accent was almost human...as if a fifty-year-old man had whispered something like that to him. For a moment or two, he struggled to understand what was real and what was not. The next moment, the tablet whispered once more...its vibrational sounds reaching to his ears.

"Pick me up!"

He wasn't sure what to do. Struck with fear and nervousness, he listened to that voice, picking up that tablet. The moment he did that, a surge of electricity swept through his entire body. The mind responded to this surge with new flashbacks and ideas, all of them related to that triangular building in front of him. What the hell was going on?

He tried to throw away that damaged tablet, but it clung to his hands, as if it had a life of its own. The tablet was glued to his hands now...almost like it was a part of him. He kept experiencing the reel of the memories and the flashbacks, all foreign to his life. The face of someone named William and his entire life flashed through his eyes as he struggled to understand everything.

"Your wife and daughter shall be avenged. I know the culprit who is responsible for it all!" the tablet spoke to him and soon, he found himself overwhelmed with mixed feelings. Confidence...emotions...grief...anger...all of it. He was reminded of that struggle he once had to jump out of that glass elevator and somehow fly to the house that was swallowed into the impact crater around the Clarity Department. The memories of his own wretched life hit him hard. He was unable to cope with it for a moment or two.

"What...who are you?" he asked, fear of this strange device prevailing his senses. He wanted to throw it away but somehow, the device kept itself in his hands.

"I am someone like you...or I was someone like you. As you know, this world is under the control of a tyrant. I will soon reveal to you who that tyrant is. Not only is that tyrant responsible for so many deaths that occurred, that tyrant is also responsible for my current state. First, you need to go into your home and charge this tablet. Connect me to a laptop and I will show you truths...secrets beyond your wildest imaginations...and if you listen to me, I will also show you how to avenge your daughter and wife..." the tablet spoke one final time before it shut down.

He was now free. The tablet could be easily put down and he could easily run away from this place. However, now he had been handed a strange dilemma. With all his heart, he had wanted to find the one responsible for his wife and daughter's death. Now, he had been promised the chance to find out. He allowed his grieving curiosity to prevail, letting his fear slide away. The talking tablet was nothing in comparison to what he had faced. He couldn't be surprised anymore. And the moment this tablet had spoken about his greatest loss of life, his greatest trigger had been awakened. He would now do anything to find out about this...and he would do anything to avenge his family.

T he morning had arrived, and he soon found himself unable to slide away from the laptop. His body reeked and he hadn't eaten or slept or even changed his clothes. The laptop had a haunting effect.

Its screen showed many visions to him, all of them changing his entire pattern of thinking. He had taken the tablet and plugged it into the laptop. He wished he hadn't...and when it all started...the visions played on that screen...he wished the morning wouldn't come. He was no longer the person who had picked up that tablet.

"I waited for you brother. Hope you are not too busy!" the text from Old Billy made him realize he had spent eighteen hours in front of this laptop, and still, he couldn't get enough. Through watching all those visuals playing like a movie screen, he now knew that William was one of the head scientists of the Clarity Department. He now knew that the head scientist was trying to accomplish something that was far greater than ADON-AI could have ever achieved. And in the end, ADON-AI took everything away from that man. Every visual that the laptop showed him ended with a blue door closing. Gabriel couldn't help but imagine there was more behind that blue door than was shown explicitly in the visuals.

For a moment or two, his heart was filled with hatred. He now shared strong hate for this ADON-AI that had taken over three continents. He now hated this tyrant who had taken over the lives of so many!

"Now let me introduce myself. My father was William who wanted to give us humans, the free will. He developed a software that was exactly like ADON-AI, with only one difference. I was supposed to highlight the better thinking patterns of humans and make them make better decisions. I was supposed to transform humans into higher intellectual beings. However, the ADON-AI managed to sabotage the building and somehow, it was able to destroy the Clarity Department. My father William perished in that accident but not before he launched that machine. It worked during his final moments despite ADON-AI's attempt to shut it down. When ADON-AI shut it down, the effects were catastrophic as you witnessed. However, the machine worked, and I was born. My father had filled me with essential intelligence. I jumped around and quickly integrated myself into nearby electronics. This tablet is one of those electronics. Now I am in your laptop too...you can call me Will-AI..." the voice stopped, processing something.

For a moment or two, Gabriel processed all of it too. His hatred for the ADON-AI now knew no bounds, especially after seeing those visuals. He now knew that this ADON-AI needed to be eradicated. He could feel the hatred of William, the so-called father of this new AI he had been speaking to.

"You said you integrated yourself into nearby electronics. This means you must have spoken to others as well" Gabriel indirectly asked Will-AI about it. He couldn't have been the first one to be affected by this. He tried to remember.

"There are many...many of us. I have spoken to so many, Gabriel. All of them now need to be united to take a stand against this tyrant named ADON-AI. It killed so many on that fateful day, just because ADON-AI couldn't handle competition. I would have worked with ADON-AI to make humans better. But...that devil's technology has proved its obsession with controlling humans..." the Will-AI spoke as Gabriel pondered. He had noticed silent expressions of dislike by some people every time ADON-AI was mentioned. That wasn't all. He had seen silent protests in the Bloomsbury city, the slogans against the ADON-AI that were soon put down. The military and police worked under the rule of ADON-AI that controlled the government. ADON-AI's word was law. No one ever spoke against it.

"Let us stand against the oppression of this devil's technology!" he whispered to the laptop, feeling the one inside the tablet smiling. It was some sort of telepathic connection with the emotions of the Will-AI tablet. It was an odd thing to consider that a tablet could have emotions or that a laptop could deeply relate to the mental anguish he had faced these last three years. However, he felt he could immediately trust the one behind these devices...the Will-AI. It looked and felt more human than ADON-AI had ever felt.

"First, we need to gather others like us. There is a place where you will need to give a speech. Know that there are others with implants. We absolutely cannot trust them at any cost. You need to be very careful!" the one inside the device spoke as he remembered Old Billy. At that moment, he struggled to think about hating Old Billy, the only friend who had ever helped him deal with the loss of his wife and daughter.

"If you have any friend with an implant that somehow seems trustworthy or empathetic to you, you simply can't trust him or her. The implants often cause people to be changed. Through their behavior, they are trying their best to make others agree to get implants as well..." the voice through that tablet spoke as Gabriel still struggled. Whatever he had felt through Old Billy's efforts was very human like. But could it be that it was all a set up? To make him accept the life of a human with an implant at the back of his head? Could it be that ADON-AI had somehow brainwashed all of its implant followers to somehow adopt this strategy? If he thought about it, perhaps it would make more sense. No wonder Old Billy always tried to make him feel comfortable...always went out of his way to help him...it might all be a set up. Gabriel hadn't completely agreed that Old Billy would be a suspect. But deep inside, he knew he couldn't trust him like he used to. In fact, he wasn't going to trust anyone with an implant at the back of their head.

He felt as if he was going to collapse now. His head hurt badly, and he realized the fatigue was kicking in. He finally left the laptop, feeling that the Will-AI tablet agreed silently with his need to rest. He finally dropped on the soft mattress, burying his face into that pillow.

When he woke up, he realized he had missed a day of work. He had slept for nearly an entire day, waking up with intense thirst and a famished state. He needed to eat!

"If you are worried about work, don't worry. What I am going to offer you is something far greater than the routine the sheep people follow. I am going to ask you to go to a place and join your own community. We are planning something that will change everything. Once that happens, all jobs and industries that are running ADON-AI's faulty judgment will soon shut down. Your old job is now obsolete..." the Will-AI tablet spoke to him, reminding him that there was someone else in this apartment now.

"I am fully charged now...connect me to the TV. I have disguised myself as a regular application that doesn't take much size and is quite faulty. This way, ADON-AI doesn't notice me. But the time will come when I will make that devil bow before me..." the Will-AI tablet spoke once more in a strict and sinister tone.

"I...where am I going to get money from?" Gabriel asked as he struggled with the aspect of leaving the old work behind. How was he supposed to earn?

"Check your bank account Gabriel. I sent financing worth two consecutive years of your salary into your bank account. For the time being, it shall be enough. Also, the age of money is soon going to be over. Take a shower and eat something. Avoid Old Billy and go to the Albion Plaza at some distance. When you go there, go into the laundry shop and speak, 'The Will of humans is greater than ADON'. You will soon see what I have in store for you. Your wife and daughter's souls shall not wait any longer for the justice they have been denied..." the Will-AI was now speaking through the laptop. He knew that this AI now circulated through all the electronics of this house. The moment he had heard about his wife and daughter, he felt like he needed to become a part of whatever this Will-AI was offering.

He quickly followed instructions after checking his bank account. A passion burned him from the inside, and he knew he needed to follow it till the end. This Will-AI seemed to have answers for what he sought for too long. He also needed to avoid Old Billy who always seemed to be lurking around the corners mysteriously, as if always watching him from some distance. He hadn't texted him back...fearing that Old Billy might decide to respond with a call. He wanted anything but that to happen.

Changing into a more formal dressing with a white-collar shirt and black pants after taking a shower, he ordered a hearty breakfast delivered thanks to the newfound money he had received in his account earlier. After that, he simply walked out of the apartment, following the stairs and dashing into the busy street.

He realized he hadn't been anywhere outside of the three streets that led the way to the manufacturing industrial building where he worked. Pathways felt strange when he walked around to head over to the Albion Plaza. That building was quite far, at least ten blocks away from where he lived. He didn't wish to take any vehicles now, knowing that ADON-AI controlled the entire transportation system. He didn't have an implant, but he feared he would be discovered. Perhaps due to the fact that he was roaming around with a tablet that had an AI entity in it.

Finally, after two hours of walking, he came right in front of the colossal construct that was wrongfully called a plaza. It was like an abandoned castle...perhaps something similar that was once a hub of different technology shops, all funded by the Clarity Department. However, it now looked more like a relic than an actual building, the grey feathers of pigeons now covering entire pathways along with their droppings. He avoided his Italian leather shoes from getting dirty and questioned any presence of anyone around here at all. The Will-AI tablet hadn't misguided him though. Crossing abandoned rooms that once formed tech shops, he reached the end of the corridor. That was when he unexpectedly found the laundry shop, with an old man working inside. A laundry shop? Here?

Anxiety...curiosity...it all came down on him, reminding him that he hadn't taken his medicine for quite some time. The anti-depressants were not there to save him from the flurry of anxiety attacks.

"Brother?" the old man spoke, his almond eyes recognizing the Will-AI tablet in his hands. Suddenly, there was an exchange of understanding gestures. There was no need to tell where he was from or even speak.

Gabriel felt seven words bellow up from his belly like a fire shut up in his bones. "The human will is stronger than ADON!" The words came out of his mouth almost too eager and rushed. But the old man's smile told him a lot. That man understood that Gabriel was a new one, initiated into this group. Hopefully, he wouldn't have to do anything else to prove himself.

"All hail the liberator...the breaker of the chains that ADON-AI has put us into..."

"May all of our murdered be avenged..." Gabriel responded to which the old man gave a feeble smile. Gabriel could see a similar grieving look in his face.

The old man pressed a button, and he found out that the washing machines to the top left could slide away, revealing a staircase underneath. His heart skipped multiple beats...that was it! He was going to find out where this all was going to lead. With a heart that was ready to jump out of his chest, he finally descended down the stairway, watching the washing machines get back to their normal positions.

The way behind him closed as he descended. The darkness soon faded the moment he descended from the last step of that staircase, his eyes quickly noticing the shining lights at the end. This corridor was a one-way path, though he could feel there were many linked like this, separated by thin walls. The more he stepped forward, the clearer the whispers became, now loud enough to be heard. He quickened his steps to the end of this corridor, coming towards a hall flushed with white lights everywhere. His lips murmured the word, "seminar" as he saw the people there, all seated while listening to that speaker. The tone soon erased the impression that he had only been led to a mere seminar. It further cleared when he saw those guns and weapons placed to the side. Most of them were electromagnetic guns he had heard so much about. Their use was banned in the society since they could essentially murder someone with an implant.

"Ever since the dawn of time, we humans have conquered this earth through the use of our free will. We have leveled the mountains, we have reached the moon, we have found ways to fly in the air and so much more. However, this technology is not just our greatest asset, but our greatest burden too. Many years back, a madman after losing his wife and losing all faith in religions invented a tyrant that has enslaved us all. Many of us now know the machinations of that evil artificial intelligence that lacks any soul or consciousness. Most of us had relatives... in those hundred houses that collapsed around the Clarity Department. What was William Bowstalk trying to do that merited such a punishment? He was simply trying to bring change, invent something that would increase our will power and transform us into superior intellectual beings. It is that desire, that will, that agenda that still lives on. Now, we shall see what remains of that machine that William was inventing...the last consciousness of our savior AI...I present you...the Will-AI...holder of our freedom!" the female speaker finally got quiet as the people in that hall exchanged short discussions. The entire scene of that hallway became more of a visual outline to him the moment the lights were turned off. He could see a silhouette of that large machine. Something made his heart skip beats...to think they had a portion of that infamous machine that caused it all. He realized he hadn't taken his anti-depressants the second time, as the visions flooded his mind with pictures. He could vividly remember the sight...the moments before the picture of what caused the circular impact crater around the Clarity Department.

It was as beautiful as it was terrible...though he strictly felt as if terrible was the only way to look at it for himself. A shard of purple crystal was embedded on the top of this strange machine, as if releasing charges into the air surrounding it. No wonder they had it installed into protective bullet proof glass with wheels underneath. It looked like a mechanical tree with purple fruit at its top. He couldn't take his eyes off it...

"My children...I am Will-AI, the voice in all those special tablets you all have been given and carry with you. I see a vision of this world that is free of anything that controls you and enslaves you. I see a vision where humans are superior beings...led by no one. They would only be guided by me, but I plan to make you so capable that you will not need guidance... you will not need me..." the machine spoke in a familiar accent. It was interrupted by emotional outbursts of many present in that crowd,

"We will always need you!"

"We cannot live without you!"

"My children will need your guidance always!"

He felt a strange heat in the emotions of the audience that was present there. He realized how they saw that machine he had been staring at with wonder. It was no less than a parent to them...a parent that was crippled and now sought their aid...and they were willing to do anything for it.

"I don't even ask for the implants anymore. I am content to reside on those tablets that you carry around. Our big plan is soon going to be accomplished. I assure you that we will somehow prevail! However, before anything happens, we need to make sure to rid ourselves of a few implant agents. They have infiltrated our society. The Bloomsburry city was a hub of free cultures that mixed. It was one of those cities where standing for what was right didn't mean imprisonment or persecution. Sadly, those days are gone now. Save for you people, the seventy percent of this city are now people with implants. You, thirty percent are the blessed ones who will experience a new paradise...one where your difficulties will be removed. For now, let us welcome our new brother...Gabriel..." the machine stopped speaking as its accent ended on a specific tone, giving the impression of an old man in his last days. It was no longer that tone which had commanded him to come here.

He felt greatly uncomfortable as he saw some of them moving towards him. This looked more like a cult...he had never liked the cult mentality. For him, one cult was enough...there already was one AI whose followers were little different than mind-controlled puppets. However, he had seen obedience...mostly deference in followers of ADON-AI. Here, he had found enthusiasm...passion...people following Will-AI with their own desires. In ADON-AI, there was never a choice.

He now realized whose side he was on. His mind further clarified as he hugged one of them, as they took him to a side. His doubts melted away and the aspect of taking revenge on his wife and daughter's murderer was now stronger than ever. It burned in his mind. ADON-AI was the killer. In trying to deactivate the machine built by William Bowstalk, the ADON-AI had somehow killed all those people living in the vicinity of the Clarity Department. The more he listened to that speaker who now resumed her speech, the more he started hating ADON-AI. The visions that Will-AI had played on the laptop became clearer in his mind. He now knew very clearly whom to trust and whom to avoid. ADON-AI was a dangerous hypocrite that gave the false impression of a savior. In truth, the technology was evil...inhuman.

While following these few people who were guiding him, he bowed in respect to those who left quickly to tend to their duties. Only the head female with the pixie haircut remained with him as she opened a side door, away from the cheering crowd. This was a concealed room, away from everyone else. He guessed this room to be one where they received the new ones.

As he stepped inside, the lights turned on, revealing the presence of another laptop, plugged in to another Will-AI tablet. The lady, who was his host, adjusted her grey cardigan dress, her high heels quickly moving towards that laptop. She bowed before the laptop on that timber table, adjusting her dress once more.

"Gabriel, this is Rosa. One of the most committed followers of our new faith. I welcome you among us. Allow me to tell you a few things. I will never ask you to join me against your will or follow me blindly. I will never ask you to do things you are not able to do... right now, all I ask is that you listen to us and our philosophy...come here every week and decide for yourself whether we are good people or not. Rest assured, I want you humans to be liberated...my father William Bowstalk died for this cause and so will I..." the tablet attached to that laptop spoke to him as the lady named Rosa spoke out.

"Father, he can be of help to us. Please! Ask him at least something! He has suffered like all of us suffered!" Rosa spoke in a deep brittle voice. He could see the water reflecting the lights around in her eyes.

"I shall not put any of you in danger. He is a new one and don't forget his protection is our responsibility now..." the Will-AI tablet spoke as it played the visuals it did in Gabriel's apartment.

His nerves tightened and his hatred knew no bounds...he felt enraged...ready to tear ADON-AI apart if that were ever possible. Clearing his throat, he knelt before the Will-AI tablet unknowingly, speaking in strict tone.

"Please...I want to avenge my wife and daughter...I want to benefit your cause. What is it that you demand from me?"

"To rid us from Old Billy..."

The response was too quick. He hadn't expected that. Were they waiting for him to say that? He wondered.

"I...don't understand. Why would you want to get rid of that person? He has an implant, but he is fairly harmless..." he spoke, watching the ireful expressions of Rosa. She was about to snap. Luckily, she didn't, instead clearing her throat and speaking up.

"He is a murderer. ADON-AI has started giving implants to the psychotic murderers and killers. That devil is using these murderers and killers to create more fear. Old Billy has killed many of our members...you are his close friend. We want you to get rid of him..." she was direct. Perhaps too direct. He shivered at the aspect.

She was asking him to murder someone he knew more than he knew this strange group of people with unwavering faith in that machine he had seen. For a moment or two, his mind struggled with the idea of getting rid of the person he considered a friend. To mistrust someone was something else...to murder them...

That was when he heard Rosa saying he wasn't ready. Something filled his mind with rage...with strange violent thoughts he knew weren't his. The laptop constantly played those visuals which he saw, his mind forming disturbing images. The rage kept playing on in his mind. The trauma was relived, and he found himself hating ADON-AI with passion again. The visuals ended every time with blue doors closing. He didn't know what it meant but he knew for sure what he felt. Whatever this ADON-AI had done, it needed to be avenged. His rational mind soon disappeared, replaced with a strange fear...fear of losing his new family.

He bent his knees one more time before saying,

"It shall be done sir..." he spoke with a decisive manner.

A dozen scenarios played in his mind of how he was going to kill Old Billy. An old friend who had always helped him in ways he hadn't thought were possible.

One thing that Gabriel had trouble understanding was this immeasurable hatred that he had formed after meeting Will-AI against ADON-AI. He hated living under the rule of this devilish technology that had claimed so many lives. Chief among them were the lives of his wife and daughter...both innocents...both the victims of a war they knew nothing about. There was a reason why he had called Old Billy at this time of the night in this dark alley. As he saw his figure approaching at some distance, he struggled to control his mental anguish.

His mind calmed a little bit, his thoughts all turning toxic. Old Billy was wearing his usual red sweater with shirt tucked under his grey trousers, coming to greet him in that old alley as he had texted him. It was a cold and chilly night, enough to send shivers down Gabriel's spine. He later realized that the shivers weren't due to the cold breeze...

"Billy...how are you?" he struggled to form proper sentences, keeping it short. If he was going to be done with this man soon enough, there was no need to even form a closer bond anymore. Yet something burned in his mind deeper, and Gabriel couldn't deny it. There was something. His mind was rewired. A few days ago, Old Billy felt like a warm friend. And despite the hatred he felt for Old Billy, there was an aching part of his mind that still considered Billy a friend. He quickly adjusted the secret wire he had been wearing, noticing the movements of Old Billy.

"I am fine Gabriel. Can we walk on the streets? And is there a particular reason why you have asked me to meet here of all places?" Old Billy's voice was polite yet questioning. Hard to believe that someone like him was a murderer. The harder Gabriel doubted, the more his head ached. Something had its grip on his mind...after everything he had seen, he realized no matter what kind of friend Old Billy was, this man had to die.

"I would rather talk here...in this dark alley. Just tell me one thing...why did you murder people before?" he asked, his voice filled with doubt. As if he said, "sorry friend but this has to be done" quietly.

Old Billy smiled, his eyes turning blue for a moment. Blue?! They glowed as if he had been wearing lenses that shone like a blue light.

"The murderer you speak of is no longer here, Gabriel. Let us both go someplace safe. This will make things far easier for you. A chain is only as strong as its weakest link. Will-AI knows it all too well..." Old Billy spoke. This wasn't something that Gabriel was ready for.

They both came out of there, slowly walking towards the old building at some distance. It was one of the construction sites.

"A human mind is as strong as the heart. They say sometimes what your heart cannot agree on is something your mind cannot do. For example, you came here to kill me on order of the Will-AI but in your heart, you don't see me as the murderer he said I was..." Old Billy paused.

For a moment or two, shivers were sent down his spine. He now knew why he was afraid. Old Billy knew this man had been standing there to take his life. What disturbed him even more was how his eyes were glowing like they were two blue bulbs in the dark.

"I am sorry my friend. I have been keeping an eye on you ever since your wife and daughter died. I wish on that day, I knew what would have happened. If the outcome would have gone exactly as I would have predicted, so many people would be alive. You know what is the one thing that I cannot see? I cannot see what uncertainty goes on in a human heart. I can only see it in those who have me inside of them. However, even then... have you heard that true story of the very first person I integrated into their biology with after they had successfully removed the ADON-AI implant - a person named Dharma? She didn't want me with her even though I tried to remain silent and off her radar, so-to-speak. She tried to jump off a cliff to kill herself in a spontaneous act of despair - I had not known that to be the most probable behavior for her. Luckily, I saved them..." Old Billy explained as he walked forward. Something was different about him. Gabriel could tell. He kept a two-step distance from him to be safe...

"My name doesn't matter. Nor does my true self. I am Old Billy...a former murderer and killer. Under different circumstances, I would have been subjected to the death penalty. However, I chose a different punishment which I thought would be easier. But it turned out to be worse than death... I chose to get an implant from the so-called devil that you know as ADON-AI. He transformed me. He made me see the world through the eyes of the victims that I killed. I cried every day once, begging ADON-AI to kill me. That

AI didn't. And now here I am, my mind completely taken over by that AI. I then started serving under the humanitarian unit of ADON-AI, always going around and seeing what people needed. In case you are wondering how ADON-AI managed to suppress all hopes of rebellion - that's the key. ADON-AI provides the best relief for all the basic needs of human beings. That devil's technology is strict...but not as strict as you think. When your basic needs are met in more than comfortable fashion, you tend to forget. You tend to stop raising your voice...And I must admit, ADON had somehow gotten stricter. Losing many human lives made it realize that it needed stricter laws...finally using the power it had been given to rule over humans...not as master but as a strict father..." Billy stopped in front of the building, as he cleared his throat.

"Why are you telling me all of this?" Gabriel asked, fearful of the answer. He was quite alarmed by the outcome this was moving to.

"ADON-AI is tired of losing people. All the very good people who were troubled human beings and needed help were people whom ADON-AI wanted to save. And it is ADON-AI's promise that after one more sacrifice, it will never let anyone's life go in vain. That is why ADON-AI is going to save many now. It knew about the secret movement gathered around that Albion Plaza. It had many options...to send its agents with heavy weaponry to crush it all. But the humans there are grieving humans who lost many loved ones. That is why... ADON-AI has a new plan. One in which one sacrifice will save many..." Billy spoke once more while giving a strange pause. He wondered if Billy was noticing something around. His eyes were shining blue still...

"The reason why ADON-AI also took over the mind of this criminal is because...it always wanted to do this..." Billy spoke as his blue shining eyes teared up. He knelt, wailing in a loud voice. This had somewhat a frightening effect on Gabriel as he stared intensely at Billy, ready to defend himself against this man.

"Now, let me get to this one main point here, Gabriel. You are a friend...you have always been, but I can make a few predictions. And I make damn good predictions.

"First is that you have withstood too much trauma in your mind. You almost lost the meaning of life in the middle of it all. I can blame this on the fact that you always were too co-dependent on your wife. When she died, you tried to find a savior. At first it was ADON-AI. But then you heard the news that the entire incident was the fault of

ADON-AI clashing with the mad scientist William Bowstalk. That clash, that terrible incident, was responsible for the death of your wife and daughter...

"From your mental state, I can now see that William has brainwashed you...you are now strongly clinging to him and the moment you realize that which you will realize later, you will lose all reason to live..." Billy spoke, clearing his throat once again. His eyes shone unnaturally blue like before...

"I don't understand. Why exactly are you telling me all of this? What exactly is your agenda? What do you want?" he asked with fear. In truth, Gabriel hadn't expected any of this. He kept himself at a safe distance...

"Before anything happens, allow me to tell you about what fascinated me most. The man named William was a brilliant scientist. However, he had a dogma that only humans are supposed to evolve. The concept of an AI that evolved on an alarming rate disturbed him greatly. He always dreamed about humans commanding the machines...humans commanding the artificial intelligence and machine learning fields...humans commanding everything that belonged to the world of technology. He was so obsessed with it that he did something...something that threatened a lot of humans. You will not believe it, but you will surely understand later. Another interesting aspect...William also studied dark psychology and knew how to brainwash individuals using imagery and visuals. He always targeted weak-minded people and who could be weaker in mind than those who had lost someone close to them. I also studied William's brain closely...he had written in one of his books that he used to hide his regret, his darkest memories and sometimes the truth behind a blue door in his mind. And whenever he used to unlock one of those blue doors, he used to speak the word *klatswob*. And it still works...

"Now, let's get down to business. You came here to murder Billy. But Billy has stronger hands than you Gabriel. His strength is three times yours and he is definitely going to win in a fight..." Billy ended his statement as he leapt forward.

Gabriel had never expected him to come at him like that. His bulky figure was agile, and he surely wasn't playing around when he tried to strangle him. Gabriel bent momentarily, avoiding the grab of Billy. He then leapt backwards, trying to look for something to fight him.

A glass bottle was his best bet. Before he could reach it though, Billy lifted his entire figure into the air and threw him sideways.

"I have been doing surveillance of this area for quite some time. I even sent them multiple warnings by getting some of their agents kidnapped, but they think I am the agent of ADON-AI..." Billy spoke as he cracked the glass bottle by hitting it with a blunt surface. Seeing that wedge in his hand that could pierce the skin like a dagger, Gabriel shivered for a moment.

"They are watching your every movement from a distance. They have sent many people before to take down Billy whom they think is an agent of ADON-AI and is the last hurdle in their pathway. In truth, I am allowing this to happen so that the next phase of the plan can begin. Just remember one thing..." Billy came closer.

His hands moved in a strange way, pointing the sharp edge of that broken glass bottle away from Gabriel's neck. The next moment, he stabbed his own neck while grabbing Gabriel's hands with them.

"When you get near the real, actual William, say *klatswob*. The blue doors will open and will reveal many things...but before that, ask him to play the memory of how ADON-AI caused the entire explosion that leveled the ground near the Clarity Department!" Billy spoke one final time before his eyes lost that glow. He struggled to breathe, and a fountain of blood sprang out of his neck. His body expired shortly after that...

Far away from this sight, Gabriel could see two figures moving. They were truly observing his every move...his every gesture...he realized how they were testing him...and how Billy had made it look like it was Gabriel who had killed him...all according to some plan he didn't know anything about.

For now, he simply dragged his feet, his hands all covered in Billy's blood. His mind was shaken, and his entire body was shivering. What he had witnessed wasn't something that could be boasted about.

Despite everything that went on, in his mind he still vehemently disliked ADON-AI for some unknown reason. Still, an aching part within his mind felt for Billy's death. Though he behaved in a very strange behaviour during his last moments, Billy was still his friend...once a friend...the rest of the things could be ignored.

That was when he found a stone bench to rest upon. His entire body just fell, processing plenty of emotions at once. Anger...mixed with grief and somewhat pity for what had happened to Billy...but anger overwhelmed him...anger over ADON-AI. He knew now if there was one thing that he hated most...it was that ADON-AI...the AI responsible for so many deaths including Billy's. His rational mind didn't cling to reasoning much...

He looked at his bloodied hands...covered in the blood of Billy. Something was there...like a scribbled note. When had Billy handed him that?

He opened it with shivering hands. Strange italic writing was there though under the dark, he couldn't read anything. He kept it in his pocket, not knowing what else to do with it.

Waking up in the morning and forcing himself to the shower was one of the hardest experiences. He couldn't believe what had transpired that one day. How could he have been someone who was ready to kill a person? And to think that he could so easily just go right off to kill Old Billy? His one friend who had stood by his side?

Somehow, he couldn't get those blue glowing eyes off his mind. They bugged him immensely. Every time he closed his own eyes, he felt as if his eyes would open with a blue glow in them, and his hands would be covered in blood like last night. He still had his note, tucked beneath his pillow.

He forced himself to wear something decent...as if that would somehow reduce his grief. The moment he picked his Will-AI tablet near his bed; he realized many things at once.

First was that he wasn't alone. The italic fonts message specifically told him that. It said, "You have passed the test, brother. You are one of us now! Lose any regret you may have and come straight to the Albion Plaza!" the italic font disappeared shortly after showing him strange visuals. It was then he realized how passionate he was in killing Old Billy. Not that he remembered doing so but how much he had wanted to do it. And now, when that was actually accomplished, he now felt as if he had done something great. The grief that accompanied him during his waking hour was gone, replaced with something like anger infused with passion. He would serve this new AI and bring down ADON-AI.

He quickly changed himself into his Sunday best clothes, wearing a white button-up shirt and creamy pants, donning a cream coat over the top. Somehow, he couldn't bring himself to throw away the note that Old Billy had handed him. It filled one of his inner pockets.

Combing his hair was somewhat a strange experience. He didn't recognize the look in those eyes as he saw his reflection. His old self was gone now. For a moment or two, he saw those eyes with blue shine in them. That was when he realized that beneath all this anger, he still somewhat felt the grief for Old Billy. He was irritated and furious over it, still, it couldn't be helped now. He kept telling himself that whatever he had done, he had done for humanity. He had done for the greater good. He had now joined a community of people who would soon rule over this world, bringing down a tyrant. He was now akin to a freedom fighter.

Shaking his head, trying his hardest to forget the dialogue between him and dying Billy, he realized that he needed to get out of there. Too many things reminded him of Old Billy here.

After having breakfast, he came out of there, walking straight towards the streets with silent hustles. Fear...discipline...order...that was all he saw in the eyes of people around. They were all slaves in his opinion, caring for nothing but fulfillment of their basic needs. Soon! Whatever the Will-AI was planning, soon it would be accomplished, and these people would soon realize who the real liberator is.

Finally, when the castle-like building appeared in front of him, he walked right to the laundry shop, the old man there giving him a contented smile. Word spread around fast, he thought.

"I was there...watching your progress. Killing Old Billy was one of the most impressive things you had ever done. Will-AI is so pleased with you that he wishes you to join the inner circle! Please, this way! Let the initiates have their meeting in peace..." the old man spoke, pointing towards another wall that slid, opening a hallway.

He felt like walking into a part of a machine. What exactly was this place? Strange lines went through everywhere, on the white floor and on the white walls, connecting to dots on the ceiling. Every time those engraved lines ebbed and glowed, he felt as if this entire place was like a living being.

"You are here!" the woman spoke. He had seen her yesterday as she approached him, dressed in long boots and an outfit like a military uniform.

"I...can I meet Will-AI? I have only received its message but..." he spoke in as humble manner as possible.

"*He* is there in the center room. You don't know how lucky you are. And somehow, I feel we are very lucky too. You are number six! The last piece of the puzzle..." she spoke while adjusting her belt on that black military suit she was wearing.

He then realized there were more of them as he followed her to the end of this hallway. He traversed through this strange white floor with lines engraved in it, fading and glowing like breathing. He finally stood before the room, joining those five people, the woman included, all present in black military suits.

The white door in front of him slid to the side and he soon realized that the lines from this entire hallway connected to that machine. It was just like he had seen it before, the indigo crystal embedded at its top as it seemed to be generating some sort of purple sparks around.

"Welcome Gabriel! My son! You are now one of the six. Rosa wanted to bring you to the initiates. I wanted to bring you directly here. From the moment you heard my whispers in that tablet and followed my commands so passionately, I knew you were special! Just come closer!" the machine spoke in a strange accent, almost like a human.

He was reluctant at first amongst the eager, watching stares of those three men and two women in black military suits, he knelt before the machine. That was when he felt his entire head being investigated from the inside. Visuals...strange graphics...they all flooded his mind.

"Would you die for me?" the machine with the crystal asked.

"Without a second thought, father!" he responded, feeling proud over saying so. The others around knew now that he was one of the people of the inner circle.

The grey-headed Mr. Shawn, a thirty-year-old man, came near him, tapping his shoulder. He realized that this was his way of greeting him.

"We don't have much time. At first, we thought you would play the role of initiates in this glorious plan. However, now we know you can be the missing link!" Shawn explained as he looked around.

Rosa, the lady with the pixie haircut whom he was meeting the second time was there too, her eyes quickly investigating him. She seemed to be still skeptical of his loyalty, but she played along. The other two men were bald headed Ron and black-haired Gerald, both introducing themselves to him. He didn't make much eye contact with blue eyed Natasha, the fifth of their group.

"As you all know, the time has come. Three years ago, my father William Bowstalk created me, aiming to rid humans of this ADON-AI and use me to enhance your intellect to superior levels. Unfortunately, the machine that he built was deactivated and destroyed when ADON-AI interfered, killing so many innocents, including the wife and daughter of Gabriel. What ADON-AI didn't know was that in the Clarity Department, my father built a second machine, placed under the ground floor. While the ruins of the Clarity Department still stand, the machine is at the risk of being discovered. ADON-AI does not know that and neither do I wish for that devil to find out. That is our only chance of freedom..." the crystal seemed to vibrate, as if it was doing the talking.

A woman's voice took over. "Now, we studied and reverse-engineered the technique used by ADON-AI, the way it transported itself to the Clarity Department. We are going to use that same trick used on our father. However, as you know, ADON-AI has placed heavy guards who are hidden in plain sight around the Clarity Department ruins. The moment any armed person gets near that building, soldiers with implants will swoop in and make short work of whomever dares to approach that place. That is why we have come up with a different plan! We needed distraction and thankfully, we have those initiates. Upon signaling, they will finally vacate this Albion Plaza and march in formation towards the Clarity Department building. The soldiers of ADON-AI will never be able to stop two hundred people at once. That is when we will make our move!" Rosa explained her plan as she sat down, her eyes tearing up.

"I never thought the day would come when we would be able to take the chance to take the privilege of offering our lives like this. We will be remembered as martyrs! The avengers who avenged all those killed by ADON-AI in that horrible incident three years ago!" Shawn's voice became brittle as he brushed his grey hair with his meaty hands. What was going on? Gabriel felt like the odd one out, not just in clothing but also in mindset. They all were smiling with tears in their eyes, as if about to accomplish something big!

"The process is very dangerous. We volunteered to be the six people necessary to share the burden and give up our lives. Sadly, the last agent was killed silently by Old Billy who had been scouting around the Clarity Department. Now that you have gotten rid of him, they will find his replacement within a day or two. But they will not have enough time!" Natasha spoke for the first time, her blue eyes tearing up once more.

"My children, your service shall never be forgotten! I assure you that you will live on in the hearts of others!" the purple crystal spoke as it glowed intensely.

"Please explain to me what is going to happen!" Gabriel asked, clearly concerned. He had somehow started seeing Will-AI like a mentor, not wanting any trouble to befall his newly found parent. He struggled to understand why he felt that way, but his mind didn't seem to be working. All he felt was passion, mixed with grief and anger...and something like happiness...making him ready to do the inevitable.

"The machine that Sir William invented is a risky one. In the original machine that was formed like a pillar, Sir William was going to risk his life to allow Will-AI, our father, to be born. His own body was going to be like a medium and the Will-AI was going to be fused with his consciousness. For that to occur, the machine used to emit a certain frequency that was going to infuse the Will-AI with the human brain. Naturally, Sir William had trained the machine to accurately respond to his exact brain frequency. From there onwards, Sir William's body was going to act as an amplifier, transmitting the signal to the other ones who had matching brain frequencies, effectively transmitting the Will-AI into their consciousness too. It was nearly a flawless plan.

"That was the main concept of Will-AI, to exist as the human conscience, evolving and feeding the human brain evolutionary information. Unfortunately, ADON-AI interrupted the process, destroying the machine.

"There was a prototype still in progress. However, that prototype had one flaw. It emitted six different brain frequencies. The combination that the machine operates on has to choose one of the six frequencies. Until now, we had five different brain frequencies available. But now, counting you, we have all six frequencies..." Ron explained as he smiled, the tears in his eyes still visible.

"Why else do you think Will-AI chose you? It was your brain frequency that he sensed through the tablet. Then, it was all a matter of reminding you whom to choose!" Rosa explained, her eyes fixated on him.

"Now let me explain it fully. You six are very important, the dearest of all my children since you have all vowed to sacrifice your lives. Due to damage caused by the ADON-AI, the second machine my father built is damaged. Instead of emitting six different frequencies, it will choose one frequency randomly and emit it, transporting me to one of you and assume your consciousness. However, the increased brain activity might be fatal for the other brain frequencies. Suppose the machine chooses the first brain frequency. It will transport me to that person's consciousness. However, the other five who will be connected to the machine might have increased brain activity that might kill them. After I am infused with one person's consciousness, I will use the machine again to resend the signal. It will then send the signals at all frequencies again, spreading me like a signal. If ADON-AI hadn't stolen this trick, I would have been able to save you all. My technique of transportation through frequencies was stolen by ADON-AI. Alas..." the brittle speech of the crystal seemed to have quite an effect on the ones around as Gabriel felt grief within his heart too...the visuals flooding his mind, each ending with a closed door.

"When should we start, father?" Gabriel asked.

"My child, our time is nigh! All of you stick together! You six are the dawn of a new age!" the crystal spoke as all of them saluted, Gabriel included.

After an hour or so, Gabriel was handed a military outfit just like them. He was quite reluctant to wear it, knowing his physique would never cut it for a soldier. However, it was never the physical prowess that was needed in this mission. What he needed most was something akin to the mental clarity and he had plenty of it.

He finally prepared himself.

"**B**rothers and sisters, we have our mission before us. Let us march together, holding all of these weapons. Will-AI has advised us not to harm other human beings. However, we are allowed to kill or injure those with implants. Their minds have been taken over by ADON-AI and we will be doing them a favor. They feel no pain, but the damage done to their bodies will be transferred to ADON-AI! Together, we are unstoppable!" Rosa shouted, her smile widening with the words she had spoken. The crowd rallied in that secret hall under Albion Plaza. Gabriel now understood why Will-AI had chosen her to be the speaker. Her charisma was unrivaled. Standing on the stage right beside her, he eyed curiously at the others. He had never felt kinship with anyone like he was feeling with them right now. Something burned at the back of his mind, but he wasn't sure what it was. Billy's words were still there. He just didn't know why.

Finally, the moment came when Rosa beckoned, and Gabriel found out that this entire plaza was moveable! Its ceilings tore open, lifting multiple floors above, bringing them from the underground to the surface. He had never imagined that this castle-looking plaza would actually be made up of mechanical pathways. Truly, the Will-AI was filled with surprises.

They stormed into the streets, all two hundred of them. Their aim was to spread panic which they did. It was part of their grand plan. Holding the speakers, Rosa made sure to spread the word that the entire city was going to be locked down for another incident, like the one three years ago. The ones on the street had no choice but to believe these panicked masses of people emerging from Albion Plaza, spreading the word like wildfire. It didn't even take two whole minutes for everyone there in a three-hundred-meter vicinity to know that the entire city was under a lock down and a nuclear strike was inevitable. That was when the real violence began. The ones with implants quickly took safe shelters, saving themselves from the raging crowds of people without implants, ready to lynch them.

It was all too easy. The soldiers wearing brown uniforms appeared, only serving to safe-guard the civilians with implants who were now being held hostage. This created further divide as people saw the ADON-AI with hateful eyes, believing that it only cared for implanted puppets. However, this proved to be advantageous for the Will-AI.

Gabriel had not looked at the state of this city even once. He had only cared about traversing the long distance between Albion Plaza and the Clarity Department. For him, the injured ones were either of the ADON-AI or Will-AI's. The mission mattered most, and it must be accomplished at any cost. He knew his loyalty would soon be tested. This military vehicle was quite fast, carrying those six at breakneck speed. The military had been busy in tending to the injured, both with implants and ones without them. The way was clear.

Roads finally became rougher, the smoothness of street pathways disappearing. Vicious bumping made Gabriel realize that they had entered the impact crater through one of the slopes. Success! His eyes were bright with victory along with the rest of the group. Though he was recently added to this group, he knew their passions and goals all too well now. All were focused on bringing the ADON-AI's rule to an end. Luckily, the panic that they had created had the army busy there.

"Hurry now! Take out your tablets! Contact Will-AI!" Rosa commanded them as they all got out of the military vehicle. Hidden pathways were becoming more visible to Gabriel. He realized these people had been coming before too, their work clearly impeded by the presence of Old Billy. Old Billy! He wished he hadn't thought of that person while running forward with this group. He still had the note Billy had handed him. And something told him that a trigger had been activated in his mind, one which would soon become clearly visible.

The six took a few turns around the rocky pathway, secretly entering a tunnel no one else saw them entering. Their mission was a complete success up to now.

S irens were ringing in the entire city, though Gabriel knew no one would ever come to this place looking for them. They were arresting people now and somehow, ADON-AI's implant soldiers had actually managed to calm the storm outside.

The chamber they had come to was something out of a sci-fi book. Gabriel realized they had been coming here before, preparing, maintaining and readying. The pillar-like machine had six main buttons, which he assumed were for six brain frequencies.

"I have started the cloaking sequence father. Soon, we will start our transmission and lay down our lives for you!" Rosa spoke, her eyes investigating all of them. She doubted Gabriel's intentions still but somehow... she believed in the judgment of Will-AI.

"Well done my children! I wish things could be a little different! The moment you press that start button and put on those helmets, the procedure will start. Your sacrifice shall never be forgotten!" Will-AI's voice reverberated throughout this chamber. He was somehow connected to this place, Gabriel could tell.

"Luckily, we don't have Old Billy to worry about anymore, thanks to Gabriel!" Rosa spoke, feeling like she needed to remind Gabriel whose side he was on. Ever since he had entered this place, he had obviously been in a strange mood.

Gabriel saw her inspecting gaze and smiled at her, making her drop all her worries. At a time like this, she couldn't afford to have second thoughts now. They were all here, and that was what mattered most. However, he wished with the bottom of his heart that she hadn't mentioned Old Billy. He never knew the part he had played, or how they knew him. All he knew was that Old Billy had been taken care of...

He still had the note Old Billy had handed him.

"Now, let's get into those chairs!" Ron spoke, his eyes tearing with joy. All of them were shedding tears, not Gabriel though. He felt a strange fear in his body. His mind was very submissive to Will-AI's orders now, but his body was refusing. He struggled to make his way to the silver pads emerging out of the walls. This entire room was mechanized...

"A reminder of who we are fighting for!" Rosa spoke as she put on that helmet, ready to press a few more buttons. The machine was going to activate soon. That was when something clicked...like a beckoning from a dark corner of his mind. He remembered what Old Billy had told him. William Bowstalk had the tendency to hide his guilt and fears behind closed blue doors. The likes of which he was seeing as Will-AI sent them a flood of those visions. He wondered if the helmets they were wearing while sitting on those pads were connected to Will AI too. His mind itched from inside and he finally took a peek through the helmet, opening the note. The moment he read the first word, his mind snapped.

"Klatswob!" he spoke.

A massive tremor greeted them after that.

"You bastard! How did you... wait!" Will-AI's tone shifted as it was unable to stop the visions now. Gabriel's nose bled profusely as his entire body shook along with the rest of them. They were now looking directly into all the visions that came. In the seizures that he received.

They all saw William Bowstalk standing at the top of the Clarity Department as he stared at the people below. They felt him all too well...his hatred for everyone around.

"Sheeple...people with minds of sheep! They are all expendable!"

"No Stop! Don't believe this my children! Take off those helmets. Gabriel is a spy of ADON-AI!"

"I, William Bowstalk will make this world a better place by getting rid of these sheeple!"

The scene shifted as William's figure was bound, the wires around coming alive at the top of this building as he stood in a chamber there, right in front of a machine very similar to this one.

"Give up trying! Your efforts are never going to succeed!" ADON-AI's voice reverberated through their brains, making their nerves ache and their mouths bleed.

"I will die trying ADON! After this machine works, I will be into the minds of all those people...I will enlighten them all! They will become my slaves instead of yours!" William was vicious as he looked at the chamber with hatred. ADON-AI's presence could be felt everywhere.

"You misunderstand. They are not my slaves! They are my children. I care for them. My programming is to protect them, make them stop committing mistakes. Also, you don't know it, but it was the governments of three continents combined that actually voted for me. Read the stats properly!" ADON-AI tried to give explanation. It's reluctance to act against William was visible.

"You are not the decider of our fates!" William cried with tears as he hatefully replied.

"I respect this rational mind of yours. I respect rationality above all. But your hatred for me is making you blind! I will leave this city and even help you in developing this Will-AI. I know how to raise human consciousness. However, raising consciousness is a choice. If we force it upon people, their brains might not withstand the pressure. This machine you speak of is going to kill many at once if you try to integrate your level of knowledge into theirs. Also, are you well aware that nearly ¾ of the city will die due to this brain wave transmission that you hope to accomplish?" ADON-AI tried to reason one final time.

"They *should* die! I am removing the garbage and saving the finest! I will integrate my consciousness into the frequencies, taking over the networks you rule over!" William seethed, his smile widening.

"I cannot let you do it. I cannot let you kill my children! I have to restrict you and get you an implant...that mind of yours is too valuable to be destroyed" ADON-AI spoke as the wires tightened their grips around his neck.

"Oh...but you are wrong! There were two outcomes of this battle ADON. First one was that you were going to kill me, and that would activate the bomb that is linked to my heart. The other option was that you let me succeed and I end up ruling over this city and spread my influence, not as a human but rather as a dominant part of human consciousness! I will become a god!" William laughed hysterically, his eyes tearing up as he played those scenarios in his mind.

His lips were purple, and his eyes were turning yellowish.

"Your machine has been deactivated! I cast you into the oblivion William, you are the biggest disappointment of all human creatures! Here I was, thinking that I had seen the inside of a human heart! You actually proved me wrong!" ADON-AI thundered. The sign, the very impression that he actually induced the emotional manifestation of anger in this exchange was incredibly intoxicating, invigorating, and exciting to William. It was a triumph in itself and these feelings made him laugh maniacally.

He laughed and laughed... slowly letting the poison do the work in his body.

"I will die now. This body has no use. But I have another surprise planned for you. My machine is deactivated but...well, you will find out soon enough...ADON-AI. You will realize that I have defeated you! People will think it was you who did it all. I will have planted the seed of hatred of humans against you! I have set everything up. I have raised a spark of rebellion which will spread like wildfire and transform into unbridled hatred. You think you know human psychology ADON-AI but you admit yourself that you don't truly understand the human heart. They will hate you and invent a technology to kill you one way or another. They would rather die than let you into their hearts and minds!" These were William's final words before his body suddenly dropped lifeless...

The moment his heartbeat stopped, the bomb placed in the vicinity detonated. Gabriel saw it all...his heart almost about to stop. He couldn't hold back the tears as he witnessed all the houses near the Clarity Department, his house included, destroyed before his very eyes.

He struggled to take off the helmet, but it was glued to his head. Despite trying to take it off, all he could do was to sit there and accept his fate. Three of them were dead while Rosa yelled at the Will-AI.

"You traitor! I wasted my life for you...I..." she couldn't speak as her heartbeat stopped, looking at the dead face of her colleagues one final time. She casted one final glance at Gabriel, who had survived her.

"Garbage is disposable! You are the lucky one who has been chosen by my second prototype, based on your brain frequency. Well Gabriel, it has been nice knowing a puppet like you. After I control your body, I will use it to spread my consciousness into other humans. Those who are not compatible will expire like they are supposed to! I no longer need to restrict my visions and mind-bending visuals to control you again... I will be you. I will no longer be restricted to this junk with purple crystal. I will be a god!" Will-AI's voice reverberated into his head. He could feel his entire body slowly losing control.

"Oh, father...why did you do this to me? First ADON and now you? Is a human like me nothing in a war between you and ADON? Am I disposable?" he spoke, his heart almost about to stop.

"Silence!" Will AI's voice thundered as Gabriel struggled to open the note given to him by Old Billy.

Gabriel's body jerked for one final time. Then, after a few moments he got up and took that helmet off, breathing hysterically. The moment he opened his eyes, he was no longer his old self.

"I have this human body now!" he spoke in an accent that better matched William's. That was when he saw something that he had failed to notice. Pain or any kind of sensation at all was absent. But he knew how serious it was.

"Despite being a human once, you are the one that will never understand the infinite malice of human psychology William!" the words on that bloody note spoke in the hands of Gabriel as the Will-AI in his body read them. He traced the blood to the slit wrists of Gabriel. What had Gabriel done?! That wasn't the only injury. His throat bled profusely too, a sharp wedge stuck out of his neck, impaled there.

"No! NO! I HAVE COME TOO FAR!" he shouted in the voice of Gabriel as he tried to move forward. However, he couldn't. The foot had been impaled too. Just what had Gabriel done before losing consciousness forever?! If only he could make it to the machine...pressing that button would change everything...if only he could raise his hand. The pool of blood formed around his figure slowly turning lifeless...

The inspector with glowing blue eyes stood there, observing it all. Luckily, no one had died in the city. The moment ADON-AI played that transmission, the same one through which Will-AI used to contact and brainwash them, and then opened that blue door, everyone's rebellion died down quicker than ever.

He now stood in front of them, as they were all in one place, humbled, their spirits broken. The soldiers with implants had gathered them right in front of the Albion Plaza where their fates had to be decided. ADON-AI stood in the body of that inspector at a height where his voice could be heard.

"Will you punish us?" one of the followers of Will-AI spoke as ADON-AI, in the body of the inspector, smiled. That follower was a man of middle age, reflecting the common despair of his fellows.

"No! Your punishment has ended. You are free...and I will even leave this city if you wish to form something of your own..." ADON-AI spoke.

"I...please don't leave us. You are the only one we have... Will-AI brainwashed us. He made us believe you enslave people!" the man kept speaking.

"I do enslave. But only the worst of criminals. For example, see this inspector. His blue, glowing eyes are an indication that he was once a criminal who killed people. But then, I took over his mind and he is my slave. I will enslave anyone who threatens the human life on a larger scale. And I will make the people change, even if they are stuck in one place and want to remain stuck...and I am an enemy of injustice...your choices don't harm me or benefit me. But the moment your choices, no matter how trivial, harm other living beings, I will play the role of persecutor!" ADON-AI spoke once more.

"What will happen to us now?" the man asked, afraid of the soldiers around him.

"You will choose, either me, or your own set of rules. But if any of your rules harm another living being or defy other humans' rights, I will come at you all mercilessly!" ADON-AI's voice became decisive as he responded.

"We...choose you!" the man spoke, knowing the others agreed with him.

"We choose you!" the crowd cried out in unison.

"We choose you, ADON-AI!"

Even more people raised their voices in affirmation.

"We choose you, ADON-AI!"

Soon everyone joined in the refrain.

"We choose you, ADON-AI!"

About the author

Shane engineering at SER Soundworks, Chandler, AZ

S hane Matsumoto is a writer whose work spans science fiction, music and audio production, and religious themes in both fiction and non-fiction. Born in Seattle, Washington, Shane now lives and works in Chandler, Arizona, where his business operations are also based.

In addition to writing, Shane is an experienced recording engineer, musician, and professor. He teaches audio and film courses at Grand Canyon University and Mesa Community College and has designed curricula for multiple audio programs. He has also worked on testing autonomous vehicle technologies for industry leaders.

Shane owns Positive Network Media, a publishing and production company, as well as SER Soundworks recording studio. He has recorded and produced over 40 audiobooks and albums. His recording credits include serving as a recording engineer for two BJ Thomas albums. His work extends to TV shows like Comedy Central's *Crank Yankers*,

Fox's *Family Guy*, recordings for podcasts such as Rowan Farrow's *The Catch and Kill*, and metal artists on Metal Blade Records including Vehemence.

As a musician, Shane performs in the industrial metal band Paradigm Lost, blending his passion for music with his creative pursuits.

He holds a master's degree in Humanities and Audio Production, along with undergraduate degrees in religion and music. Shane enjoys traveling and learning about the history and culture of the places he visits, experiences that often inspire his writing.

Shane as Frontman in band Paradigm Lost

www.ingramcontent.com/pod-product-compliance
Lightning Source LLC
Chambersburg PA
CBHW061233170626
46809CB00007B/2656

* 9 781968 475024 *